KAYLA WREN

Their Mountain Bride

BLACK CHERRY

PUBLISHING

Contents

Keep in touch with Kayla!		iv
1	Angelo	1
2	Beau	7
3	Katy	13
4	Angelo	19
5	Beau	25
6	Katy	34
7	Angelo	42
8	Beau	49
9	Katy	58
10	Angelo	66
11	Beau	74
12	Katy	83
13	Angelo	91
14	Beau	98
15	Katy	105
16	Angelo	117
Teaser: Autumn Tricksters		121
About the Author		127
Also by Kayla Wren		128

Keep in touch with Kayla!

Want to hear about new releases, sales, bonus content and other cool stuff? Sign up for Kayla's newsletter!

1

Angelo

Almost a year.

Almost a year, I've been with Beau Walker. Scratching out some rustic living on the mountainside; breathing in wood smoke and dressing in stiff flannel shirts. The baggy, checked monstrosities that I wear now are a far cry from my wardrobe back home in the Marino mansion.

Back there, I wore silk. Cashmere. Tailored suits and hand-tooled brogues.

Here, my boots are a size too big. I keep balled up socks stuffed in the toe.

At first, I barely noticed the way Beau lives. I was too injured—dazed and bashed up by the river, my skull knocked about and my muscles pulped under my skin. Then, when I finally started to heal under Beau's care, I was dazed in a different way.

Back home, even when I was sick, no one *tended* to me. Not beyond the barest medical needs. Sure, my father paid people to nurse me, but I creeped them out. There were too many stories about me. So no one went the extra mile, brushing my forehead or pulling my blankets up to my chin. They scuttled in and out of my quarters, spending as little time in my presence as possible. Trying not to catch my eye.

Beau was a revelation.

Even if he did it all with a scowl.

So it took me until deep winter to notice how fully shitty it is on this mountain. I guess I got wrapped up in Beau's grumpy charms and let them distract me from the fucking wasteland he calls home.

I mean, there are wolves and bears and hidden ravines. Storms sweep through the valleys without warning, and there is a perilous rock slide at least once a month. No sane human person would come to Lonely Mountain, look around, and stay.

Beau must be crazy.

Another reason I keep him around.

Case in point: not once has Beau asked what I was doing here before I fell in the river. There have been no casual questions, like, "Hey man, were you fishing?" or "Lost your hiking group, huh?"

He plucked a man half dead off the river bank, nursed him back to health over several months, then said nothing when that man made himself at home and refused to leave. Beau just built an extra room onto his cabin for me. Like he was buying in a different brand coffee.

See? *Insane.*

And it's not like I've been holding back, either. Back home, I'd go through these phases, especially while I was growing up, where I'd try to act *normal.* You know, mimic all the right manners and facial expressions.

Smile. Laugh at a normal volume and at appropriate moments. *Blink.*

Human stuff.

It didn't work, obviously. I still freaked them all out, so badly that if I weren't a Marino, some asshole would definitely have dragged me into an alley somewhere and put me down. Even my father couldn't look me in the eye without turning pale and sweaty—not for long. Only my brother Dante could, and look how *that* turned out.

Chasing him here. Winding up in the river for my trouble.

Caring is no fucking joke.

So I've stopped pretending. First, I was too injured to put it on, and then when Beau didn't freak out and make me leave… well, why would I? Sure, the people in town don't like me much—they visibly shiver when I stare at them; their breath catches when I smile—but they're all too scared of Beau to say anything.

They won't run me off with pitchforks. Not while I'm with him.

Funny, really.

Beau's a pussy cat.

A scarred, mangy mountain lion of a pussy cat, which only communicates in grunts and snarls. He's an odd one, yes, but who am I to talk?

He saved me.

And now he's *mine.*

* * *

The Mountain Rescue cookout shatters our domestic bliss. I should have known it couldn't last—Beau's willful ignorance of where I came from. The lightness in my chest. The sense of *peace* that came with no one knowing a goddamn thing about me or my family name.

Angelo Marino can't have nice things. Not to be a little bitch, but that's the way things are.

I suppose I tempted fate. I've been getting bolder—going into town with Beau for errands. Visiting him at work in the Mountain Rescue headquarters. Wandering around the library when it opens late on Thursday evenings, staring openly at the pretty blonde librarian, then hiking back up the mountain in darkness with my blood rushing in my veins.

I haven't exactly been flying under the radar.

But seeing Dante... that is a punch to the chest.

Beau's working the grill. Being the big, manly man, the stoic provider, and though I murmur teasing comments to him, I can't pretend I don't enjoy it. Especially when he rolls his shirtsleeves to his elbows, his forearms light brown and scarred, corded with muscle and dusted with dark hairs.

Beau may be a rough bastard, but he is a well made one. Sometimes I stare so hard, my eyes run dry.

The cookout is busy, for the low season anyway. People are laughing and chatting, milling around on the lake's edge, and the grill hisses and spits, the scent of cooking meat drifting through the air. It's early in summer, still a cold bite to the air, but the locals sun their pasty arms and legs like we're on the Med.

They muster their courage before they approach Beau at the grill, thrusting out open buns like he might tear their arms off. He serves them without speaking. Or *maybe* with a muttered greeting if he knows them. And they dart away with their food as soon as they humanly can, giggling nervously to their stupid friends.

4

God, this town is pointless. Dante was onto something—our father would *never* look for us here.

I lean my back against the side of a brick building, watching the crowd under half-lidded eyes. I've never been a smoker, but now seems like the exact perfect moment to light up. It would be something to do with my mouth, with my *hands.*

The other thing I want to do with my hands glances over, raising an eyebrow in question. Beau waves at the sizzling meat with his tongs, and I raise one shoulder. He can bring me food if he likes.

Beau rolls his eyes, but he snags a bun off the nearest table. Flips it open and selects a burger.

It's the best one. Ah, Beau.

I never get my food, of course. Because that's the moment that they approach, slipping out of the treeline and wandering down the lakeside. My brother walks shoulder-to-shoulder with his companions, closer than he ever walked with me, and he's relaxed. He's *smiling.* With the breeze tugging at his dark hair, and a blue checked shirt stretched over his shoulders.

Disgusting. I drop my imaginary cigarette and grind it beneath my heel.

I should never have come here. To a town event, for fuck's sake, with an open invitation for all who live on the mountain. With free food, and chilled beers resting in ice buckets on the fold-out tables, and the strains of some tragic acoustic music floating across the crowd.

The Dante I knew would not have been caught dead here.

But I don't know my brother anymore, do I?

My Dante would have nothing but scorn for this ridiculous cookout. *My* Dante would bankrupt this town sooner than live near it.

5

But this Dante is no fun—a tasteless wretch like the rest—and when I see him, my heart thumps faster. Not with fear. I'm not *afraid* of the asshole. But unlike last time we met...

I have something to lose.

I don't tell Beau I'm leaving. There's no time, not with Dante bearing down on the crowd, his eyes curious and searching. I push off the brick wall, squinting up at the bright sunshine like I've suddenly remembered something, and drift casually around the corner out of sight.

A stranger leaving the cookout early.

Nothing to see here, folks.

My strides pick up as I cross the bare dirt, small stones crunching beneath my boots, and I wipe my palms on the front of the denim monstrosities I now call clothes. The wind's picking up, lashing against my stiff cheeks, and it'll toss plumes of grill smoke over the crowd if they're not careful.

Perhaps Dante will catch a chill and leave.

Perhaps he'll remember he hates charred meat.

Or maybe Beau won't notice the family resemblance. Our shared dark hair and sharp eyes. Dante's paler than me, after all, and he looks entirely different when he smiles. We're not *that* similar. Not carbon copies or twins.

Maybe nothing will come of this.

If only I believed in luck.

2

Beau

What kind of fool lets a man live with him without asking a single question?

It's my fault. I don't ask questions because questions lead to answers, and that is dangerously close to chatting. But I feel every inch of my stupidity when the dark-haired stranger approaches the grill. Because I *know* those quick eyes. That pointed chin. I stare at that face more than my own.

It's Angelo. Or Angelo-adjacent.

It seems my mystery hiker has a past.

"Burger or hot dog?" I grind out the question, my throat tight and itchy from breathing in the dark smoke. The man orders three burgers, his words clipped and imperious, even when he remembers to thank me.

Yeah, he definitely knows Angelo. He's a spoiled little asshole too. I glance around to call for my... whatever he is, but Angelo's gone. Slipped away while my back was turned.

So, okay. Guess it's down to me.

"Visiting town?" It's the most I've chatted with anyone all day. The man nods briefly, his mouth pressed in a line.

Not a big talker either. Usually, I'd appreciate that.

"You know Angelo?" There's no other way to ask it, so I blurt it out as I hand over the first burger. The man takes it from me, but I don't miss the twitch in his fingers.

"Angelo?" He clears his throat, voice box bobbing. He's paler than his... what? Cousin? Brother? Long lost twin?

"Yeah." I lower my voice and the man moves closer, drawn in though his mouth twists and his eyes are wary. "You look just like him. Spitting image."

He nods. Licks his lips. "Yes, I—yes. Angelo, huh? Is he here?"

I frown. Or, well—I frown harder. The last decade or so, my face has been set in its ways. "What? You don't know?"

He *does* know him. And what are the chances of two relatives just turning up on Lonely Mountain? So why this dance? I don't follow.

And why hasn't Angelo mentioned someone coming to visit? If he had, I'd have made myself scarce. Left the social stuff behind and gone to the summit for a few days.

If he makes me sit through some tearful reunion, I'll kill him.

"He's staying in my cabin." Living there, if I'm honest with myself. "You gonna drop round?"

"Maybe." The man nods slowly, like the thought only just occurred to him. "Maybe I will."

Okay. I'm tapped out. This conversation is happening somewhere above my head, and I don't like shooting the shit at the best of times. I press the third burger into the man's hands, nod once, then turn back to the grill. Prod the meat with my tongs until he takes the hint.

When the man shoulders his way back through the crowd, my shoulders slump. What a weird guy. He even leaves the burgers piled on a table, out where they'll go cold and attract dogs, then grabs his two friends and drags them back along the lakeside.

I watch them go, tongs held loosely by my side, the grill spitting for my attention. And I can't even be pissed about the ruined burgers—it's all too fucking strange.

The hairs stand up on my arms.

There's something Angelo's not telling me.

Scratch that—there's *everything* Angelo's not telling me. I used to appreciate that about him—hell, I wouldn't let him stay if he talked my ear off—but now it looks like something is off. Badly wrong.

And I can't get mixed up in something. People already piss themselves when I'm near. I can't give them a real reason to fear me.

I toss the tongs onto a side table and gesture for someone to take over.

Angelo has some explaining to do.

* * *

"There was a man at the cookout."

I don't tiptoe around it. As soon as I'm back at the cabin, I shove the door open and start talking. Angelo's perched on a stool at the breakfast bar—the one *I* built him when he whined for it—and he turns to me with a serene, blank face. Even halfway up the mountain, his red flannel shirt and dark jeans are spotless.

"A man? Beau, there was more than one man there. Women and children, too. But good job—what else did you spot?"

God, he's an asshole. Why do I keep building him shit? I slam the door shut behind me, the floorboard creaking under my feet as I stride closer.

Angelo's hand shakes as he picks up a mug. But he sips from it, humming like we're at a fancy cafe, not my scruffy cabin.

I scrape a hand down my beard.

"There's something going on." I gesture at him vaguely. "I don't know *what* but I know that it's off. That man looked exactly like you. Like a brother or something."

"Mhm." Angelo lowers his mug with a soft thump. "So what I'm hearing is, you're seeing me everywhere."

"No—"

"Hallucinating me. Hearing snippets of my voice. You must really like me."

"*No.*"

"Then what?"

"I don't..." I pinch the bridge of my nose. There's a flush creeping up my neck, I can feel it. "I don't know."

This always happens. I get tangled up in my thoughts, tripping over myself. But I had a point—I *did.* Because there was a man at the cookout who looked like Angelo, and Angelo took off early without telling me. That was weird.

And the man seemed shocked to hear Angelo's name. He *also* took off early.

That was weird.

It's not the first time I've looked at my new lodger and felt... unsettled. Like there's something prodding at the back of my brain. Something I should notice. But that feeling has always gone away before, so I never had to ask him about it.

"So you don't have a brother?"

Angelo's face clouds. For a split second, he looks bitter. And his words are clipped when he says, "Not anymore."

Well, shit. This is why I don't ask questions. Why I mind my own business. Because when I ask questions, I ask the *wrong* ones. I put my foot in my mouth. I drag up bad feelings.

I should drop it. This conversation is already giving me hives. And though we haven't talked much, though he's an unsettling kind of guy... I like Angelo. Or something. We have a kinship, a bond that comes from saving someone's life, and more than that—we have comfortable rhythms. He's like a mouthy piece of my furniture.

But that alarm bell's still ringing in the back of my brain, and I can't let it go. I let this man into my home.

"Is there... something you're not telling me?"

Angelo snorts delicately. "Lots of things, Beau. Tell me: what's my favorite color? What's my favorite type of wine?"

"That's not what I meant—"

"We don't know the first thing about each other. Do we?" He spreads his arms, his smile knowing. "This is the longest conversation we've ever had. That's why this living situation works. Right?"

Right.

I can't argue with that. People aren't my strong suit. And for all his high-and-mightiness, they're clearly not Angelo's either. When he hangs out in the Mountain Rescue headquarters while I'm on shift, we get hardly any drop ins. He creeps people out.

He doesn't creep *me* out, but that's not saying much. Before Angelo got here, and before I started at Mountain Rescue, *I* was the town outcast.

"But if there's something I should know..."

"I will tell you." He smirks. "Or perhaps I'll write it down. Avoid this unpleasantness."

"...Yeah. Okay."

11

It's not okay, not really. I somehow have fewer answers than when I came in, and I stomped up here with my brain tangled in knots. That man knew Angelo, no way around that, and now he's sitting all prim at my breakfast bar and lying to me, bold as day.

Do I really want to know, though?

Maybe not.

We've all got issues. We've all got secrets. You don't find yourself on Lonely Mountain if your head's on straight. Ain't no one in a hundred mile radius who doesn't have *something* to hide.

Hell. I don't tell him everything. And do I feel bad about it? Not for a single second of the day.

Sometimes a man has to be let alone. Or a woman, or—or anyone. It's practically a human right, especially up here inside the cloud bank.

But I still grind out a warning as I squeeze through the doorway to the kitchen, my shoulders brushing off the wooden frame.

"Angelo?"

"Yes?"

"Don't cause me any trouble."

He scoffs, spinning his mug handle with one finger. "Or what?"

That's the million dollar question. What would I do if he caused me trouble? *Trouble*, beyond half killing himself a river, then moving into my cabin like a stray dog, that is.

In the end, it's obvious. Even though it sticks in my throat.

"Or I'll kick you out. And I do know some things. I know you got nowhere to go."

3

Katy

I hover on Beau Walker's deck for way, way too long. If he happened to twitch his cabin curtains to the side, he'd think I was crazy. A twenty-four carat stalker, with only a scuffed up tote bag of books as an alibi, hopping from foot to foot out here in the dying light.

There's no one for half a mile around at Beau Walker's cabin, only skeletal tree trunks and branches, and they're even creepier at dusk. Leathery bat wings flap overhead, the little critters zipping from roost to roost, and I draw a big, cold breath of air into my lungs.

I blow it out slowly. Count to five as I do.

Is this a bad idea? Maybe it is. Maybe Miriam was right.

The library doesn't *deliver*. It's not a pizzeria. You can't order up three hardbacks and a dictionary for doorstop drop, thank you very much. Not unless you're one of the town shut-ins, anyway.

But Beau Walker didn't try and do that. I'm the loon who brought him a bag of unasked-for books to the Mountain Rescue cookout, and I'm the even bigger loon who missed her chance to give them to him and then followed him home.

Like a puppy. Or a stray cat.

Not a grown human woman, with a job and an apartment and a full selection of cleaning supplies under the sink.

"You've done it this time, Katy." My lips are numb from the chill as I whisper to myself. The seasons may be turning, but winter holds on with a vengeance on Lonely Mountain. "You've crossed a line. People will *talk*."

My jacket zipper catches as I jerk it up to my chin. I'm in my favorite jacket, a puffy pink one, and I told myself when I shrugged it on before coming up here that at least I wouldn't get lost in the dark.

But the wind moans through the gloomy trees, the light fading fast, and there's a prickle on the back of my neck. Like maybe I don't want to be seen after all. Not out here, where the shadows shift and the leaves shiver overhead.

Beau Walker's cabin is big. Bigger than most on the mountain—probably because he keeps bolting rooms on like giant lego blocks, adding bells and whistles like there's no tomorrow. You can see where he's added new bits over the season, his hands restless or something, because the wood's slightly newer. Brighter. Not so weather-beaten yet.

One bit even looks like a small turret. That makes my cold lips curve. Because a man who builds something like that—well, he's secretly fanciful.

A man like that might read *all* sorts of books.

And I might find his client record, and see what he reads, and nearly fall off my library stool.

The windows glow orange—it's nearly full dark now—and just the sight of that glow warms up my insides. It's a flickering light, a firelight, and my brain rockets back to the memory of

14

Beau Walker manning the grill at the cookout this afternoon.

What is it about a man flipping meat outdoors that's so primal? It's like a cave woman thing. I took one look at him gripping those tongs, muscles flexing, and practically melted into a prehistoric puddle on the ground.

"Come on, Katy." The decking creaks quietly as I shift my weight back and forth, back and forth. One hand's raised, curled in a fist and ready to knock, while the bag handles cut into the other. "Let's get this show on the road. Crap or get off the pot."

The whispers don't help. After another long moment, my arm drops back to my side, and I stare at the dark front door until my eyes prickle.

It was a bad idea anyway. And this way, no one has to know that I came all the way out here, sniffing after my caveman crush like some desperate loser.

Yeah. No harm, no foul.

And no restraining order.

My tote bag bounces off my shin as I turn, the sharp book corners prodding through the fabric. I wince as the decking groans under my feet, the wooden steps bouncing under my weight, but I'm halfway to the trees before the door flies open behind me.

A rectangle of orange light spills over the dirt, pinning me in place. I freeze, heart hammering, as a rough, deep voice calls out into the night air.

"Who's there?"

My breaths are so *loud*, whistling in and out of my tight throat. I should turn, should speak, should do something, but I'm trapped in my own panic. Choking on garbled greetings, muscles shuddering under my clothes.

It must be the darkness, getting into my head and freaking

me out. The waxy full moon hanging swollen above the clouds. The little cracks and slithers audible from the shadows. Because even though I chose to come here, even though I wanted to see Beau Walker, hearing his gruff voice...

Goosebumps ripple up my arms.

"Turn around." The low command makes sweat prickle on my palms. What the hell is wrong with me? He's a man, not a minotaur.

But I've clearly been reading too many horror stories. Too many dark fairy tales about girls getting lost in the woods. Because I don't turn around and smile at Beau Walker, don't explain why I'm skulking round his cabin at night.

I suck in a sharp breath.

Drop my tote bag of books.

And run.

* * *

"Damn." Miriam, the head librarian, whistles low and long as I clatter through the library front door. Heads spin at the stacks of books; fingers hover above pages; the clicking pauses at the computer desks. "What happened to you?"

I clear my throat. Then raise my chin, as though I have a single scrap of dignity left to protect, and cross to the check out desk.

Miriam waits for me, one hip jutted out, her purple mani-cured nails drumming on the lacquered wood, and I wait for the clicks and whispers of turning pages to start up again before I speak.

"I screwed it. Went all the way up there, rehearsing some stupid speech like I was in a movie, then the second he opened the cabin door, I ran."

Miriam hums. "Yes. I knew you would."

Briefly, I consider throttling my boss. But I'd probably crease her printed blouse, and Miriam is very particular about her outfits.

"You knew I'd drop a bag of library books in the dirt and leave them there?"

Her kohl-ringed eye twitches. "Yes." She taps her temple. "I *knew*."

There's only one thing Miriam likes more than slapping late fees on tourists, and that's her wide and ingenious array of side hustles that she runs out of the library back room.

Over the winter, it was holiday-themed photo shoots, with a dress up box stuffed with reindeer antlers and Santa fat suits.

In spring, it was DIY foraging kits and hand weaved wicker baskets.

Apparently, this summer is psychic season. The tourists are coming, about to descend on Lonely Mountain in droves, and Miriam has declared them ripe for tarot readings.

"Listen," she'd said when she first pitched the idea to me, wheeling the returns cart up and down the stacks. "No one comes to Lonely Mountain unless they're lost. You know. Spiritually, or whatever."

She had a point.

And Miriam does look the part. With her halo of short curls, statement makeup, and indeterminate age, she'd be right at home on a psychic's poster.

"You didn't really leave my books in the dirt, did you?"

I slam back down to earth. Hurrying around the side of the check in desk, I arrange my face into what I hope is a reassuring smile.

"Don't worry. I'm sure Beau took them inside. And I'll go and fetch them back tomorrow."

Tomorrow, when I have to admit what a weirdo I've been.

Miriam huffs. "I ought to fine *you*."

"Probably. Sorry, boss."

There's more clucking and grousing, but we settle back into our evening routine of checking in the last of the day's returns. The rhythm of it is soothing, the quiet of the emptying library wrapping around us like a blanket, but when closing time comes around, my pulse has still not settled.

I can't believe I did that. Any of it. Going up there uninvited—dropping those books—running away like a criminal.

An hour later, I linger in the library doorway while Miriam locks up, peering up at the night sky. The stars seems to pulse, their light flaring and fading by turns.

What will Beau Walker think of me?

I've blown it. Before I even began.

4

Angelo

Beau's grumpy as we load into his truck the next morning. Nothing new there, that's for sure, but for once it's not my doing.

We had a visitor last night. A mysterious blonde book-bomber, dropping a bag of library books in the dirt and sprinting off into the trees. Beau told me about it with halting words, his forehead creased in confusion as he set the bag of books down on the kitchen table.

But as the hours passed and the fire popped and flickered, his bemusement turned to an angry scowl.

Beau hates visitors. And he *really* hates when the locals treat him like some kind of Bigfoot. He ate breakfast in a moodier silence than usual, his glare flicking to the books every few seconds. Then he stood up, dropped his spoon in his bowl, and grunted for me to get in the truck.

The vehicle bounces over the rough mountain track, never mind that Beau drives like a little old lady. He hunches over the steering wheel, glaring out at the dirt path like his mystery visitor might launch at him out of the bushes.

"It's rude."

I blink, sitting up straighter. Beau hasn't spoken for hours. Not since he told me about the girl outside his cabin, his brow creased in confusion.

"Book-littering?"

"Running away from me like that. It's rude."

I wait, but that's all he offers. It's about the average length of a Beau Walker conversation. Normally, I might fill in the blanks myself. Unlike Beau, I like to hear my own voice, and honestly, there's no one better to chat to, especially on this backwater mountain.

But it's still tense between us, still strained from the cookout, and I've got my own worries to dwell on.

Like: does Dante live here still?

Will he hunt me down? Come looking for revenge?

I need to get a gun. Not some stupid hunting rifle, a handgun. Something small and stylish that fits right in my palm. Something well made, with a delicious *heft*. My fingers twitch, already tingling.

"You think it was a prank? Some kind of dare?"

I frown, flicking at the tote bag handle in my lap. "Maybe. Who knows? The people here are weird."

Beau grunts. The truck lurches through a ditch and back onto the path.

The truth is, I know exactly who left those books. I knew as soon as Beau mentioned blonde hair and a pink jacket—the library stamp inside the top book only clinched it. Because while Beau gets absorbed by the stacks when we go there every other week, *I* get absorbed by her.

Katy Poole, the librarian. I got close enough to read her name tag once. She smelled like green apples and sunshine.

She's not the type to stake out a man's cabin on a dare. I'd bet my future handgun on it.

"What did she drop?" I dig through the tote bag as Beau drives, the truck windows fogging with our breaths. It's warming up outside, the morning sunlight breaking through the trees, but the truck's still cold.

Beau grunts again, like that's an answer.

And *he's* rude too, so I don't tell him what I find. I just read the titles, one by one, my grin stretching wider and wider. And when I find the note, I read that too, manic laughter bubbling up my throat.

"What?" Beau snaps.

I stuff them all back in the tote bag. Lean my head back against the headrest and force my breathing to slow.

"Nothing." I sound off, but he doesn't catch it. "Let's go tell your prankster off."

* * *

The Lonely Mountain town library is a tragic sight. At least, it is for *me*—I'm used to grand city buildings. Marble lobbies and pale stone steps; gilt-framed oil paintings lining the walls.

The library here has faded green carpets and laminated posters. Banks of ancient computers and an honest-to-god fax machine. Every time we visit, there's some kind of awful bake sale, with squished up cakes and cookies clustered on paper plates.

Beau always buys one. He always offers me one too.

Town Bigfoot? Please.

I spot her before he does: a flash of blonde hair ducking behind a stand of leaflets. So when Beau approaches the battleaxe head librarian at the check out desk, the muddy tote bag clutched in one hand, I shove my hands in my pockets and stroll between the stacks.

She doesn't notice me coming. No one ever does. I'm non-threatening, see? Average height, average width. Only the eyes creep people out, and by then I'm already close.

"Hello."

Katy Poole jumps up with a gasp. Her cheeks are flushed bright red, the blush splotchy where it travels down her neck. She's dressed in a plain white t-shirt and a red cardigan, her library lanyard hanging over the inviting shelf of her breasts, and her fair hair is half tied up, half down.

"Oh! Um. Sorry—can I help you?"

I peer at the leaflets she's hiding behind. *Overcoming Addiction.* How fitting.

Ignoring her question, I step closer. I only have a few moments to survey her away from Beau, and I want to test my theory. To see her before and after he comes near.

"Um. Sir?"

She's short. That's not ideal for Beau—his head scrapes when he ducks through most doorways. But she's plump, built with generous curves, and that will go in her favor. Even when Beau's gentle, he's stronger than he thinks.

Her hair looks soft. Shiny under the electric lights. And her lips part as she blinks up at me, startled and confused.

My chest pinches. Yes. Yes, she's perfect. Beau will fall instantly, with only a smoking crater left where he stands. He thinks he's hidden that part of himself well, that gooey, vulnerable center, but I've seen the books he hides on a private shelf in his bedroom.

The romances.

The self help dating guides.

I'm pleased for all of ten seconds. But then reality comes knocking on my thick skull, Beau's words from yesterday echoing around my brain. *You got nowhere to go.*

He can't fall in love. There's only one way that ends, and it's with me kicked back into the big, cold world. Back to the mercy of my father. This woman with her bag of perfectly chosen books, with her sugar-sweet note asking Beau to dinner—it's a disaster.

There's only one option: I open my mouth ready to warn her off. To spin some terrible lies about Beau. The man who saved my life.

"There you are!"

I don't get a chance. Because the head librarian rounds the stacks, her shoulders draped in patterned shawls, and Beau trails behind her, looking like he's headed for some brutal dental procedure. His mouth is pressed in a firm line beneath his black beard, his forehead is set in a deep scowl, and he won't meet anyone's eye.

With his gray shirt stretching over his barrel chest, I can see why Katy gulps, shrinking back against the leaflet stand.

"Mr Walker here brought our books back, Katy." The head librarian widens her eyes pointedly. "Perhaps you two have something to discuss?"

She sweeps away without another word, and I don't even realize she's pinched my sleeve between her fingers until I'm dragged along with her in a cloud of jasmine and baby powder.

"Hey." I jerk my arm free halfway across the library, pinning her with a dead-eyed stare. "I was watching that."

She startles at the eerie look in my eye, but she recovers faster than most, smoothing a trembling hand over her shawls.

Huh. All this time with Beau and I'm losing my edge.

"They're not a television show, Mr...?"

"Smith." I treat her to a full-toothed smile.

The librarian shudders. Good. That's more like it.

"She meant no harm—"

"By trespassing? Following a man home? Lurking around his cabin at night, peering in the windows and eavesdropping?"

The librarian puffs up like a rankled bird. "That is *not*—"

"We're done here." Beau appears at my elbow, cheeks flushed and eyes hard. "Let's go."

Over by the stacks, I catch a final glimpse of Katy Poole as she turns around. Her face is pinched and pale, her hair deflated somehow.

"You give her a hard time?"

That was way too quick for anything else. And Beau, the idiot—he nods once, sharp.

"Yeah. Now let's go."

He won't have enjoyed that. For a scary motherfucker, Beau hates conflict. On the rare nights I trick him into playing board games with me, he always lets me win. It'd piss me off, if I also didn't love winning at any cost. We're a perfect pair.

"Good." I clap my hands together, suddenly buoyed taller. This went extremely well. "Glad that's sorted."

Beau grunts. Guess we're back to monosyllables.

I wink at the bristling head librarian as we turn for the exit. And I can't help peering over my shoulder one last time, searching for a glimpse of Katy Poole.

She's gone, ducked away again, but that's okay.

I'll see her again soon.

5

Beau

Caleb gives me a knowing look the second I push through the Mountain Rescue office door. Angelo follows behind me, hands thrust in his pockets and a smug smile curling his lips.

He likes coming to the Mountain Rescue headquarters. He's claimed a sofa here now, staking out the territory like a stray cat.

My partner stands behind the scuffed wood desk, rummaging through the maps crammed on the ancient bookcase. It's a tight fit between him and the wall—Caleb Olsen's a big guy, almost as big as me, but he gets none of the flak that I do.

No jittery old ladies cross the road when he's walking near. No one calls the hotline for help, then hangs up when he's the one to answer.

Maybe it's his tawny hair. Or the crinkles at the side of his eyes that come from so much smiling.

Or maybe I'm just a big scary bastard.

Katy Poole sure thought so. My teeth are still grinding three days later, anger and something else churning in my chest whenever I think of her. The tiny librarian wasn't too scared to come and mess with me, was she? But when I loomed over her in the town library, she looked ready to pass out. Like *I* started it.

Doesn't matter. It's fine—she's just like the rest of them.

I don't care.

"Any call outs?"

My shift doesn't start for another ten minutes, but already I want to get out of here. It's too hot in this room, the warmth from the heater baking the layer of dust on the bookshelves, and I need cool air on my cheeks. Wind tugging my hair.

"Nope." Caleb slaps a map down on the desk and starts smoothing out the creases. "The season's not started yet. It's still quiet."

I know that. But is a tiny rock slide too much to hope for? No injuries, obviously. But a bit of havoc. That's what I need.

"Hello, Caleb."

I shake my head as Angelo calls out, crossing to hang my coat on the hook. He can't resist it—needling everyone he meets. Where I hate that I put people off just by existing, where I would give anything to meet someone and have them not do a double take, Angelo's the opposite. He plays up his freak factor, hams it up like a Broadway actor.

I'm not convinced he's even that creepy. Not really. It's like a defense mechanism or something.

"Hey, man." Caleb's better with him than most. Super patient. And maybe that's because he's my partner and he's doing me a favor, or maybe he's just *good.* Giving Angelo the benefit of the doubt.

It's misplaced if he is. *I* might like him, but Angelo's a dick. No doubt about it.

He's sprawled on the sofa now like a king on his throne, limbs tossed in every direction and one boot dangling over the arm. He never sits like that at home, when no one's watching. He's always neat. Contained and precise. But then, he's not trying to spook me, so.

I might feel differently about Angelo if he watched me like that. Under half lowered lids, like a cobra watching a mouse and trying to decide if it's hungry.

"Don't be weird." I kick at the base of the sofa. Angelo sits up straighter, but flashes me a smirk.

"Sorry, darling."

Heat flares under my beard.

He's wearing one of my shirts again. Angelo does this sometimes, when he's too lazy to do laundry. Just strolls into my room and combs through my clothes, like it's nothing, like he has the right to them. Rubbing his thumb over the sleeves like he's testing fabric swatches.

I never stop him, either.

And seeing him swamped by my shirt, his toned but smaller body awash in the stiff flannel, the collar open at his throat...

I cough and frown at the floor.

What was I doing again?

"Heard you had a dust up at the library." Caleb watches me out of the corner of his eye, a finger holding his place on the map.

Great.

"So everyone knows?" It's not like I wanted to cause a scene. The opposite of that. But a quiet library is not a good place to have a private word.

I know that now. Fuck.

Caleb's mouth twists. He's still not reading his map. "Katy

27

Poole's a sweet girl."

Maybe to him. Everyone's sweet to Caleb—hell, he's got a girl and a guy. *Two* people fell in love with him, while idiots like me can't even get one.

I blow out a sigh, hoping he'll take the hint. I don't want to talk about this. I don't want to talk, period. The floorboards creak under my weight as I cross the room, and I pull a crate of climbing supplies from under the desk to clean without a word.

"Beau…"

"What?"

Angelo huffs from the sofa. That quiet puff of laughter makes my jaw clench, but I ignore him.

Caleb pauses, weighing his words. But he's not scared of me—a fact I usually appreciate—so he doesn't hold back. He speaks his mind.

"I heard what happened. Bits of it, anyway. And I don't think she was messing with you, man. Katy's not like that. We went to school together."

I pluck a carabina out of the crate, turning it over in my hands and checking for damage. "What, then?"

Caleb half laughs, and that strangled noise makes me look up. He's got his palms raised, a smile playing around his mouth, and suddenly I want to punch through a wall.

I don't, obviously. No sense giving people a real reason to run away.

"She's sweet on you."

…No.

I didn't hear that right. But it's quiet in this office—especially now that Angelo's gone silent. Like he's holding his breath, unblinking eyes watching me from the sofa.

"What?" It's comes out as a grunt. But Caleb nods, his face open and almost pleading.

"Yeah. She's—she brought you those books as a gesture. That's what Miriam told Bianca who told me, anyway."

Angelo mutters something about *schoolyard gossip,* but I'm not listening.

A gesture? I screw one eye shut, trying desperately to wrack my brain, to remember some of the titles. Did I even look inside the bag?

No. Not really. I was so pissed off, so worked up at her running away from me like that, I didn't even consider the books might be for me.

Which ones did she bring me?

I've never wanted to know something so bad in my life.

Too late, I realize they're both still watching me. Staring openly at my face, waiting for me to react to the clearly impossible idea that a pretty young woman like Katy Poole would come looking for *me.*

Fuck. I must be fifteen years older than her. At least.

Am I a pervert if she started it?

No. No, this is a mistake. Caleb's not screwing with me—I know he's not like that—but someone's got their wires crossed somewhere. Pretty little Katy Poole doesn't want the town Bigfoot.

And even if she did…

Well. I blew it, didn't I?

* * *

I leave Angelo in the Mountain Rescue headquarters with a muttered excuse. Something about picking up screws from the general store. He gives me a narrow look, his pale eyes calculating, but he doesn't follow me.

Good enough.

The town square is busy at midday, the glass store fronts sparkling in the sunshine, and I weave around the locals as I cross to the library. They dart out of my way when they see me—as if I'd kick them otherwise, *get a grip*—and the nerves snaking around my stomach coil tighter.

I just want to see her. Apologize, or—or something. Clear the air with Katy Poole.

And once I see the fear and dismay in her pretty face again, I'll know for sure. Caleb's talking shit.

"'Scuse me." Sparrows flutter out of my path and conversation dies around me. I firm my jaw, shouldering past the clustered locals, and step through the library doorway.

The sudden darkness makes me blink, white spots floating before my eyes. It's not pitch black in here—far from it, with rows of electric lights flickering overhead. But compared to the bright sunshine of the town square, the library is a cave.

"Beau Walker." The head librarian—Miriam, I think—purses her lips at the check out desk. "Hello again."

This is awkward. But that's too bad anyway—there's only one library on Lonely Mountain, and I'm not giving up my books no matter how awkward it gets. They'd have to outright ban me, and even then I'd appeal.

I need this place.

I just didn't realize someone else had noticed.

"Is she here?"

No need to specify who. It's not like I've had run-ins with the other librarians. But Miriam frowns, her smooth forehead pinching.

"Katy apologized, Mr Walker. I'm not sure what else you hope to achieve."

At least this woman's not afraid of me. It's small comfort when she's keeping me from Katy, but it's something. It means I can push a little harder.

"I'd like a word."

"But—"

"Please." Apparently that really is the magic word, because the head librarian huffs then turns to peer at the stacks. She rocks up onto her toes, her chin moving as she stares, and I turn to do the same. Searching for a flash of blonde hair. Searching for *her*.

The woman who brought me a bag of books.

God, what did she bring me?

"It seems Katy has slipped away." Miriam looks far too pleased when she turns to me, flashing a close-lipped smile.

"Where did she go?"

The dramatic shrug disturbs the woman's shawls. One end drops off her shoulder, dangling to hang below the desk.

"To lunch? To the bathroom? To take cover from another of your outbursts?"

It's so fucking unfair, I could bellow like a bull. I didn't have an *outburst*, I had a quiet word, but no doubt the town gossip is that I raged and threw bookcases. I scowl at Miriam, and there's no satisfaction when she finally wilts.

"Please leave," she hisses.

Gladly.

I rap on the desk, turning to go, and only pause when something nudges at my brain. I could get one question answered, at least. This whole humiliating trip doesn't have to be for nothing.

31

"Miriam?" I double check her name tag before I speak.

"What," she says flatly. It's not really a question. She wants me gone.

"Which books did Katy bring me? Do you have a list?"

Miriam peers at me, clear distrust in her eyes. "Why do you want to know?"

And it's a good question. I made such a fuss about the books, and now I'm interested in reading them? Angelo would know what to say to get them out of her, but I don't have a good excuse ready and he's not here. I settle for the truth.

"I didn't look in the bag." I clear my throat, voice rough. "I wish I did."

Miriam watches me for another long moment, making up her mind about me. I fight the urge to scratch my cheek.

Then: "Here." She spins in a whirl of colored shawls and taps away at her keyboard. Prints off a page and snatches it up with a flourish.

"This is your customer record. Katy checked the books out in your name." She pushes the page into my hand, crinkling a corner. "She foolishly thought you might *read* them."

"Thank you." That's all I can mutter as I turn away, striding across the library carpet until I'm safely back in the town square, squinting in the sunlight but safe from Miriam's gaze.

The list is... it's something.

Like Katy Poole reached inside my brain and meddled around in there. They're books and authors I've wanted to try for years, along with others who are my all-time favorites. A personalized reading list better than one I could have made for myself. A declaration right there of someone who *knows* me.

No one knows me like that. No one except maybe Angelo—and he lives with me. Doesn't count.

32

Katy Poole has never said a single word to my face. Not until I cornered her and forced out a single one: *sorry.*

I walk back to the Mountain Rescue headquarters slowly, lost in thought and chewing on the inside of my cheek.

Katy Poole wasn't messing with me.

And I scared off the one person who wasn't afraid.

6

Katy

Well, I did it. I humiliated myself in front of the whole town—with Beau Walker's help of course. I ruined twenty-five gossip-free years in one night, and made myself a laughing stock.

They'll get over it. There are plenty of weirdos on Lonely Mountain to cause a scene, and I'll be old news in a couple of weeks. I know that, and yet I still flush bright scarlet when Beau Walker squeezes through the library entrance and two dozen heads spin to watch me.

No.

Look away, you assholes, I beg them all in my head, crouching ridiculously low and scuttling along an aisle. My shelving cart is left abandoned, blocking the stack, but it's too late to turn back. I need to get out of here, right. Freaking. Now.

I'm an idiot, okay? I got caught up in all those cheesy movies I binge in the evenings after work, and I saw the books Beau Walker checked out on his record, and I figured I *knew* him somehow. That we were sappy kindred spirits, die hard romantics in a cynical world, never mind his constant scowl.

But he put me right. I know better now.

And I don't want to wave awkwardly as he browses the stacks. I don't want anything from Beau Walker. Not anymore.

"That room's reserved," one of the elderly ladies at the knitting tables calls over. I roll my eyes, turning the handle to one of the private reading rooms nice and slow, so it doesn't squeak. Pulling it open a crack, I find it blissfully empty.

Aha!

Suck it, Audrey.

This will do nicely. I slip through the opening, closing the door softly behind me, and flick on desk lamp nearby.

The reading rooms are a throwback, designed for privacy and serious study, but you don't get a lot of either in this town. A sturdy desk rests against one wall, an empty shelf on the wall above, and two spindly chairs take up most of the floor. The window is big, stretching right across the far wall, and the glass panes are still fogged from the morning chill.

The sun hasn't reached this side of the library yet. It's cold in here, and I hug my waist against a sudden shiver.

The door opens before I can react. A man slips through, moving on silent feet, and closes it with a muffled click before turning to face me.

"You're Beau Walker's friend," I blurt.

I know this guy. He's been living in Beau's cabin since last fall. He was the favorite topic of town gossip for *months*—at first, because of his dramatic accident in the river, and after he was healed, because he freaked people out.

His eyes, they said. They're bottomless. Dead and predatory, like a snake.

The man crowding into the reading room with me, though—he's not dead-eyed. He's smirking, mischief sparking in his fine-boned face.

"Um, can I help you?"

I don't know what else to say. *Screw off* is not in my DNA.

The man takes me in, his roving gaze leisurely as it slides down my front, all the way to my ankle boots, then back up my jeans and pink t-shirt.

He smiles wider.

"Hello, Katy Poole. You're hiding from Beau."

I splutter. I *am,* but it seems rude to point it out. "And you are?"

"Angelo."

"Angelo who?"

"Angelo Smith."

Yeah, right. This guy's last name is no more Smith than mine is. But he stares at me, challenging me to call out the obvious lie, and I falter.

Crap. I'm no good at conflict.

"What do you want, Angelo?" I read once that to defuse a tense situation, you should repeat a person's name.

"I saw the books."

Perfect. Well, who hasn't at this point? Gossip travels like wildfire through this ridiculous town.

"And I read your note."

That gives me pause. Because as far as I knew, no one else had found out about that. It was the one thing I had to thank Beau Walker for—that he didn't spread it around the whole damn town that I asked him out to dinner. Right before he reamed me out for trespassing at his home.

So, okay. This guy Angelo knows. Which means what he does with that knowledge is officially beyond my control. I try very hard not to get hung up on things I can't influence. Even dark-haired things with sharp cheekbones and knowing smiles. Even extremely handsome things.

See, this is the problem with a non-stop diet of romance novels and sappy movies. You start projecting those story lines, seeing meet-cutes and swoon-worthy figures in real life, when in reality, they're just... a disappointment.

And I'm done with that. Beau Walker has officially shamed it out of me. So I draw myself up to my full, tiny height, and pin Beau's friend with a frosty glare.

"That doesn't matter now."

"No?"

Angelo leans against the wall beside the door, his arms folded over his chest. I try not to notice the way his muscles bulge beneath his sleeves.

"No."

"Why not?"

"Because Beau wasn't interested. And he was an asshole."

That smirk grows wider. And damn me, there's something magnetic about this guy. I feel the corners of my mouth tugging, trying instinctively to smile back. My heart lifts, the tightness in my chest easing, even though there's no good reason for me to find this guy reassuring.

"*I* liked your note."

I fiddle with my lanyard. My cheeks are warm. "Um. Thank you?"

"Do you know why Beau is here?"

My shrug is clumsy. Like I've forgotten how bodies work. So my quiz master takes pity and answers for me.

"He's having second thoughts. He thinks he may have been hasty." Angelo pushes off the wall, his arms dropping to his sides, and for a crazy moment my breath catches in my throat.

I've never been trapped like this in a small space with a strange man. I thought it would be nightmare fuel, not that it would make me all tickly and restless, a vivid slide show of what we *could* do in here flickering in my mind's eye. "Do *you* think he was hasty?"

"I don't…" My brain won't work. Especially when Angelo reaches out, tucking a stray lock of hair behind my ear. His fingertips linger, tracing a soft line over my cheek. "I don't know."

His hum is soft. Low. I bite down on my lip. And when he steps back, I exhale in relief, sagging on my feet.

"Beau is no good for you." The change in his tone is abrupt. From warm to warning. "Better to keep your distance."

Um, what? I stiffen, the flutters in my belly dying away in a blink. I know that, I don't need some stranger weighing in. Warning me off like a jealous boyfriend. The reality of my situation floods back in: I'm hiding at work, tucked away in a small room with a strange man who touched my *hair.*

"Excuse me." I scrabble for the door handle, yanking it open regardless of the noise. If Beau Walker sees me after all, so be it. I'm done with this conversation. "I should get back to work."

Angelo doesn't move as I plunge back out into the stacks, cheeks flushed. And when he speaks, it's so quiet, I barely catch it at all.

"Good to meet you, Katy Poole."

I snatch my shelving cart and set off, the wheels bumping over the carpet.

* * *

Why oh why am I attracted to weirdos? First Beau Walker with his scowl and his scars and his—his *shoulders*, making me go all melty with his secret romance novel addiction. That was a bust.

Then his freaky friend corners me in a small room, and instead of screaming for help, I... what? Make conversation? Smile at the guy?

Flirt?

Not proper flirting, obviously. That would require a working brain. No: middle school level flirting, complete with twirling my hair and losing track of every sentence.

Honestly, I deserve the shit everyone's giving me. I'm a mess. "Beau was here."

Miriam watches me knowingly as I drag my empty cart to the front desk. I hid out in the stacks for forty minutes before I braved coming back here.

"Oh, was he? I didn't notice."

She snorts. "You're an awful liar."

I am. Let's add it to the list, next to flirting and seduction. But the good news is, I've never publicly shamed someone for the crime of liking me.

"And what did Beau want?"

Miriam's smirk is just like Angelo's. Superior and infuriating. "He wanted to know which books you brought him."

Which books I...

I shake my head, trying to dislodge the weird cotton wool brain Angelo left me with. "...He didn't know?"

I mean, he had the bag overnight. He brought it back in person. He didn't even peek inside, not once? He could even care enough to look?

"Nope." She pops the 'p'.

"So he..."

"Didn't see your note? No, I don't think so. I don't think he realized the books were for him at all when he came stomping in here, his beard all twisted up in a tizzy. He thought you were pranking him."

Pranking him.

Pranking him.

Well, I sure hope someone is laughing.

The mischievous glint in Angelo's eye crosses my mind, and something tells me at least one person is enjoying this car crash. Inside, I warm to him again for a split second—before I remember his warning.

Better to keep your distance.

"Those men are trouble." I shove the cart in its spot next to the desk, kicking at its squeaky wheel.

"Men?" Miriam prods. "Are you talking about the man you hid with too? Men, plural?"

It's... not unheard of. Not in the books Beau and I both like to read, and not even in this town. Caleb Olsen, a guy I went to school with, is in a menage. It was hot news a while back at the knitting table.

But Miriam's quirking her eyebrow over nothing. Neither of those men like me—and I sure as hell don't like them.

"They're assholes," I say flatly. "Give me a break."

Miriam grunts, and it's so unladylike, I huff a laugh. I fall into place beside her, sliding a stack of books across the desk and lifting the scanner.

"I could do you a reading." She tugs the desk drawer open, showing me the contents. A large stack of jewel-toned tarot cards nestle among the usual post-it pads and paper clips.

"You've looked up what they all mean?"

"No. Not yet. But how hard can it be? It's probably more

accurate if it's… instinctual."

That's so not how it works. And I love Miriam, but the last thing I want right now is my boss announcing to the whole library that I'm about to meet a tall, dark stranger.

The last tall, dark stranger I wanted has caused me nothing but trouble. So there.

"No thanks." I nudge the desk drawer shut. "I'm on the straight and narrow. From today forward, no more crushes and wishing on a star and all that bull crap. No more waiting for a fairy tale. None of it is real."

Miriam sighs loudly, but goes back to scanning her own pile.

"I don't know whether to be more proud or disappointed. You were going to be my best customer."

7

Angelo

It's surprisingly hard to find my brother's cabin again. You would think, what with the way I stalked him here with a single minded obsession last year, that the location would be fixed in my brain. But the godforsaken pile of rock that Dante calls home is so *samey*.

It's all moss-covered boulders and sharp drops. The carcasses of lightning-struck trees, wrenched half out the ground. Leaf litter and the skittering sound of rodents.

Even the cabins look the same—all except Beau's, anyway. Thank god I moved myself into the only one with any sense of character. The others are all like something out of an outdoors magazine, all neatly stacked firewood under cover on the deck and a hammock slung under the eaves.

Please. It's so windy here, you'd be spun in that hammock like a washing machine.

I know when I've finally found Dante's cabin. Recognition tickles at the back of my brain, and my body reacts too. My breaths come faster, shallower, and my muscles are tensed and ready for flight.

The last time I was here, I ended up in that river.

I flick the safety off my new handgun, holding it loosely, pointed at the ground.

Leaves and bits of twig crackle under my boots. I approach slowly, circling the cabin from far away and moving closer. Closer.

It's not how I remembered. It's unkempt. There are slats missing from the cabin walls; dark shadows in the windows. I keep circling anyway, but by the time I'm thirty feet away, it's clear the cabin is abandoned.

Fair enough. I found Dante here once. And even if he thought I died in that river, our other relatives are just as dangerous.

You don't underestimate the Marinos. He's not a fool.

There won't be anything here, but I climb the decking steps anyway. For old time's sake.

"Dante." I call out to the darkened windows softly, like I'm singing. "Dante, I'm home."

Nothing.

Only the moaning wind, and the rustling trees.

I'm not disappointed. I'm not.

It's better this way. My brother and I can live on the same mountain. As long as we each keep to ourselves, what's the problem? He has those companions, the man and woman who blinded me with rage when Dante chose them over me...

And I have Beau.

Another face slides across my mind. Round, pink cheeks and blue eyes. Pearly white teeth digging into a plump lip. But that's nothing. I warned Katy Poole away, and no one has ever ignored a warning of mine before. Back home in the city, whole families uprooted at a single sharp word.

The door pushes open easily under my palm. There are signs

of life inside, alright—animal life. Clumps of matted fur and piles of small animal bones. I wrinkle my nose, pressing my sleeve against my face, and walk in further.

The stench is strong.

Dante would hate this. My brother is very particular about his belongings. He likes finery best of all, but even on this mountain, I observed that he preferred things neat. Well taken care of.

And these are *his* belongings, strewn in a panic from when he fled me. I kick out at a coffee table, the wood gnawed and scratched by dozens of creatures.

He shouldn't have fled. I wasn't *dead set* on killing him. And even if I were—I'd have seen reason. All I wanted was my big brother back.

The cool air whips at my cheeks as I stride back onto the deck, heart slamming against my rib cage. It keeps beating double time, until it's bruised and aching in my chest, all the way back to Beau's cabin.

All the way home.

* * *

Beau is reading. Stretched out in an armchair that looks ready to collapse under his bulk, one scarred hand stroking his beard as he holds the book up to the firelight. He glances over when I stand in the doorway, stomping more than necessary to dislodge the bits of twigs from my boots.

"Where were you?"

Every word from him is a rumble. I scoff, shoving off the door frame and striding inside.

"Walking."

It's none of his business. Beau goes walking more than a pampered pet dog. Just because I would normally rather stab myself in the eye than go walkabout on this tragic lump of rock, does not mean I deserve an interrogation.

I sidle around the edge of the kitchen table, my new handgun digging into my back. It's covered by my jacket, tucked safely in my waistband, but Beau's not an idiot. He'll recognize the lump if he sees it—and lord knows he stares at my ass enough to notice.

"Walking?"

The book lays forgotten in Beau's lap. His scowl is deeper than usual, creasing his broad forehead, and his gray eyes are startling against his brown skin. I pointedly avoid them as I shuffle to my room, kicking a hand-carved footstool out of the way.

"Yes. Do you know this word?"

Beau's face shutters.

Good.

He doesn't speak again as I slip into my bedroom, tucking the handgun safely out of sight beneath my pillow. And when I emerge, he's pretending I don't exist. Paging softly through his library book, his breaths soft and slow as they move his big chest under his black wool jumper.

…His *library* book.

Shit.

"What are you reading?" I cross the room and duck down, trying to read the spine, but Beau snatches it away, leading me in a ridiculous dance around his arm chair. Even sitting down, he can hold it out of my reach—and I am not a short man. "*Beau.*"

"A book," he grunts, whipping it away for the dozenth time.

45

But I catch a glimpse of the cover—a woman in a scarlet ball gown, tearing the shirt off a long-haired man.

Recognition tickles at the back of my neck. I *know* that couple. I've seen them before—in Katy Poole's tote bag.

Shit. *Shit.*

Fury and bitterness swells in me like the tide.

I warned her. I told her to keep her distance. But that does me no good if he still goes *looking*. It's all too fucking obvious where that path ends—with Katy Poole and Beau Walker playing happy families in this warm, bright cabin, and me out there in the cold and dark again. Back with my family, or worse.

"No."

"What?" Beau frowns up at me, bemused. I shake my head quickly.

"Nothing. That's one of Katy Poole's books, isn't it?"

He grunts. That means yes. So does the flush darkening his cheeks above his beard.

"You like it?"

Another grunt.

Shit.

I tug it out of his grip, too frazzled to think of a better move. Beau yells something indistinct, lunging to take it back, but I hold up both my hands in surrender, dancing out of reach.

"Stop! I'm not stealing it, you moron. We're going to play chess."

Beau pauses, half out of his armchair. Then sags back, rueful but resigned. He knows how this goes—sometimes, I just need his *attention*. Not often, but sometimes. I need it like a weed needs sunshine.

"Fine. Get the set."

But *this* is new. Usually it's me ordering Beau around like my delectable manservant, not vice versa, but I guess I've finally pissed him off enough to push back. It sets an unfortunate precedent, but I toss his library book down at a safe distance and stomp over to the bookcase. Can't let him back out now.

"You're white." I place the board on a side table and set it before his armchair, then drag a stool over. He digs in a faded velvet bag for the pieces, setting them each gently in place with a muffled thump. "Make me work for it this time."

Beau rolls his eyes, a quick flash of white, then takes a piece and makes his first move. The first few turns are rushed, my movements jerky, but after a while we settle into our rhythm. Slow breaths and the gentle *thump* of pieces on the board.

"Where did you walk?"

I scowl at his queen. Still out of reach.

"Outside."

He blows out a hard breath through his nose.

Then: "You go looking for your visitor?"

What visitor?

Of course not.

Fuck off, Beau.

The answers line up ready on my tongue. But I must be more rattled by that library book than I thought, because instead, I hear myself grate out the truth.

"Yes."

Beau pauses, his hand hovering over a knight. He's as shocked at my rare flash of honesty as I am.

"Did you find him?"

Why stop now? "No."

"Who is he?"

"My brother."

"Where—"

"Are we playing chess or are we chatting like milkmaids?" I take his rook to punish him for all these stupid questions, but it doesn't help. I'm still snarled up and fizzing inside, and I slam my own piece down so hard the board wobbles.

"Careful."

There's a note of warning to Beau's voice. A note I've never heard before. And somehow, it's like a fingertip running down my spine. I jerk upright, my skin hot and my breath caught.

The next time I move a piece, I'm more gentle.

"Good," Beau grunts, and Jesus Christ, my insides are rioting. Throwing off sparks like a wildfire.

I clear my throat, fighting to keep my face clear.

"Don't speak to me like a child."

"Then don't act like one."

My cheeks ache from fighting a smile as I make my next move.

It will be fine. Everything will be fine. Beau has already done my work for me, ruining any chance he had with sweet little Katy Poole when he humiliated her in the library. And if I can't find Dante, maybe it's because he's not here anymore.

Maybe he heard my name and fled.

Maybe *I'm* the big, bad wolf, not him.

It's a pleasing thought. The best bedtime story out there.

8

Beau

The nice thing about librarians is they're easy to find. The clue's right in the job title, and there are signs pointing to the library all over town. So catching one to talk should be an easy thing—when they don't duck out of sight every time you walk through the door, anyway.

I let Katy Poole hide from me three days in a row before I put a stop to it. We can't go on like this—not with all these bad feelings stewing in the air and an apology clogging up my throat.

I don't do conversations.

Awkward ones are even worse.

But I need to talk to Katy Poole.

That list of books she brought me… it's done something to me. Knocked something off kilter, somewhere deep in my chest. I can't—can't sleep right, can't eat, can't think straight until I talk to her. Clear the air. I read the first two books in a daze, and now I have questions.

So by the fourth day, I'm too damn hungry and tired to let her hide again. I duck through the library entrance, sunshine at my back, and blink away the bright spots in my eyes at the sudden gloom. She's here somewhere, I know she is. Hiding from me. Scared.

"Hello."

Miriam nods at my gruff greeting, leaning on one elbow at the check out desk. Bright, waxy tarot cards are spread in front of her, and her blue manicured hand hovers over the row, drifting back and forth.

"Getting ready for the tourists?" I can do this. I can chat. Especially if it gets me one step closer to pretty little Katy Poole.

"Yep." Miriam squints at me through one eye, then selects a card with a flourish. She tosses it down in front of me, and I bend down to read the writing aloud.

"The Hanged Man."

She chuckles—a rough, smoky sound. "Looking for someone?"

Alright, then. Guess we're done chatting—fine by me.

"Katy's hiding."

"Uh-huh."

"Where?"

Miriam cocks her head. "Why should I tell you that, Beau Walker?"

It's a fair question. If I heard Katy had been hiding from any other man, and her boss outed her hiding place—I'd be pissed off. A woman's got a right to hide, I would say. The man better suck it up.

But I'm so tired from not sleeping, I can hardly see straight.

"I read her books. The ones she brought me."

"All of them?"

I pause, scratching my cheek. I'm not the fastest reader. "Well... no. Not yet. Only two so far, but I'm getting through

50

them. I'm gonna read them all. And I want to ask Katy about them."

"What do you want to ask her?"

Holy hell, I'm going to do this whole damn conversation twice. If it weren't Katy Poole I was trying to find, I'd be out that door already. I force my jaw to unclench, and give a shrug.

"How she knew I'd like them, I guess."

"Well, that's easy. We have a record of all the books our customers check out—"

"—And why she came up to my cabin," I interrupt. I don't want the brush off from Miriam. I *know* that bag of books wasn't something Katy would do for just anyone.

This is special.

Or it was—before I wrecked it all.

Miriam stiffens, shoving off her elbow to stand up straight. She pierces me with that owlish glare.

"So you still think she was pranking you?"

"No."

No, damn me. No.

"You don't?" The voice is faint behind me. I lurch around, always too big and clumsy, especially indoors, and there she is. Katy Poole, hovering by a bookshelf, openly eavesdropping on every word I say.

I don't mind. Now I don't have to repeat myself.

"Katy."

Her name is foreign in my mouth. Which is funny, because it's been going round and round on a non-stop loop in my head. *Katy Poole.* So pretty. Pretty and neat, just like her. She's dressed in blue jeans and a plain gray t-shirt, the hem tucked into her waistband. Her library lanyard is skewed to one side, dangling off one gorgeous—one other part of her.

51

I cough. "Hello. Uh."

Now that I've found her, my brain's gone blank. I've been rehearsing a damn speech for the last four days, but when her big blue eyes narrow at me, I don't remember a single word.

She hates me.

And unlike everyone else, she has good reason to.

"I'm sorry." The words rasp out of me in a hurry, way too loud for this quiet library. My declaration echoes, bouncing off the walls, and heads turn our way.

Oh well. I embarrassed her in public. Guess I should do this part in public, too. My skin goes hot and itchy with all the attention, but I stay put. No going back now.

Katy's eyebrows twitch, and she unfolds her arms. They drop to her sides, dangling awkwardly.

"That's…" Her mouth twists. "That's okay."

"No, it's not." I start to take a step forward, before I remember the way she's been hiding. Just because she's talking to me out in the open now, that doesn't mean she wants me closer.

I settle for smooth a hand over my beard, staring at her like I can absorb her clean through my eyeballs.

"I shouldn't have told you off. Not without checking what happened."

The library is silent. There's no rustle of pages or clicking computer mouse—only held breath as everyone strains to hear every word.

"That's…" Katy blows out a hard breath. Her cheeks are bright pink. "Thank you, Beau."

She offers me a smile, a small, fragile thing, and I feel so good I could tear a tree trunk straight out of the soil. But then she's nodding to herself, turning away like we're done, and *no*. That can't be all.

"Dinner?" I blurt the word like an idiot. Katy frowns at me, bemused, and I force out the whole sentence. Goddamn it. "Would you go to dinner? With me? Please?"

It's ridiculous. There's a muffled giggle somewhere in the depths of the library, and I can't even blame them. That asshole is right, whoever they are—Katy Poole is young and sweet and bright and beautiful. I'm old and big and scarred and awkward. It's an insult to even ask her, really, and I'm opening my mouth to take it back when she speaks first—

"Okay."

Uh. What?

Her smile is bigger this time, though no less fragile. She nods slightly, that flush still bright on her cheeks, then blows out a quick breath before marching past me to the check out desk. She grabs a scrap of paper and a pen, writing out her phone number in rounded, loopy writing.

She puts her name on top. Like I might forget.

Holy hell.

"Call me, Beau Walker." For all her nerves, Katy's eyes sparkle when she nudges the paper into my hand. Our fingertips brush, and then she's off, walking back through the library with a sway to her gorgeous hips.

"*Well.*"

Miriam taps a pen on the desk, and I turn and stare at her dumbly. Did that just happen?

"You sure you won't take a reading, Beau?"

I glance at her cards. The vivid reds and purples; the eerie figures holding up silver swords and golden cups.

"No. Thank you."

My ears ring as I stride to the library doorway. I don't need those cards to tell me—the future's looking up.

* * *

Angelo's already in the Mountain Rescue headquarters when I arrive for my shift. He's hunkered on his sofa, his laptop balanced on one knee, clicking angrily as the screen washes his face blue.

I pause in the doorway. "Poker?"

Angelo grunts. We're not that different really.

I'll admit, I was curious what a man like Angelo might do for a job. When he was resting up in my cabin after the river, healing his bones and learning to move properly again, I tried to picture it a few times.

Angelo working a checkout.

Angelo in an office.

Angelo in a dentist's smock.

I might as well have pictured a tiger working that checkout. That's how jarring the image was—Angelo seemed more likely to be a hit man or a gigolo than to work as a teller at the bank.

But I wasn't about to pay for his ass, not after he recovered from the river. I was all set to draw a line, to insist he get out and work like everyone else and damn the awkwardness. But that conversation never happened, thank god, because shortly after Angelo recovered enough to go into town, he... *manifested* a laptop out of nowhere.

I don't know how he got it and I probably don't want to know.

But now his online poker games earn more in one night than I do in a month.

I wouldn't ask him for cash—not beyond a few dollars for food and firewood—but a big chunk lands in my bank account every time he plays. It's a pattern. He gets nervous, visibly fidgety about the idea I might ask him to leave. He'll never say it outright, but that's what it is. And soon after, a little row of zeros lands in my account.

I've told him he doesn't have to do that.

I don't think it sunk in.

Caleb leans around the sofa behind him, his eyes going wide at whatever he sees on the screen.

He whistles. "*Damn.* You picked the right hiker off that riverbank, Beau."

Angelo scowls harder, but keeps clicking. A faint flush darkens his cheeks.

"I keep the winnings. Beau is not my wife." His accent is thicker today. Another sign he's stressed.

I don't call out the lie. About the winnings, obviously. Not the other thing.

"You ask Katy Poole out yet?" Caleb throws himself into the seat behind the desk, watching me with a grin. I shrug off my jacket, hanging it on the peg, and suck at my teeth. Angelo won't look up from his screen.

"You two gossip worse than that knitting club."

"Is that a yes?"

"Yes."

Now he looks up. Angelo watches me, face eerily blank.

"What did she say?"

"She said yes. And she gave me her number." I pat my pocket, like that's proof somehow. Even though out of everyone, Angelo and Caleb are the least likely to think it's bullshit.

Angelo just keeps staring, not twitching a single muscle, not even *breathing.*

Then he blinks. "Good." His chin drops and his fingers rattle over the keyboard, typing out some angry tirade. "That's good."

The blue light of the screen hollows his cheeks. It makes

him look harsher, sharper than he really is. Still good-looking, though. Almost as pretty as Katy Poole.

The thought lands with a clang in my skull. I shake it off, pushing it to the back of my brain with the rest.

Caleb's watching us both closely, his gaze bouncing between us. He fiddles with the edge of the desk, something haunted behind his eyes.

"I said I'd take her to dinner." Honestly, I can't believe I'm volunteering more details, but it's so tense in here suddenly. The air's thick and too hot. "Where should I book?"

Caleb hums, thoughtful, but he's still watching Angelo. I look too.

"Italian, maybe?" Caleb murmurs.

Angelo's cheek tics.

Okay. I don't know what's going on here. Only that there's a second conversation happening, somewhere buried under the first, and no one told me. And one is hard enough to parse, let alone two. So screw it.

"You alright?" I direct the question at Angelo. He jerks, looking up at me quickly before staring back at his screen.

"Yes," he clips out. "I am always *alright*. Especially when I am taking money off idiots online. Why wouldn't I be?"

Right...

Right.

"Italian," I repeat. "Yeah, okay. Sounds good." My face is hot as I cross to the bookcase. I'm about to dig out some random handbook, anything to keep my hands busy, but I'm saved by the hotline phone. It trills out, shrill and loud, and I swipe it off the hook.

"Mountain Rescue. Beau speaking."

The babbling in my ear calms my nerves. *This*—this I can

handle. I grunt as the guy on the other end of the line talks about his hiker buddy, the twisted ankle, the dark clouds rolling over the mountains—

"We're on our way."

Caleb's already standing, shrugging on a windbreaker. He fiddles with a radio at his belt, twisting the dial, and I glance at Angelo.

"You'll answer the phone."

Angelo huffs. "Probably."

He will. He's just being a dick, but I can read him better than he realizes. And Angelo *likes* Mountain Rescue. He likes being part of something.

He'll answer the phone.

"There are two other crews on call tonight. If something comes through—"

Angelo waves an airy hand. I shut up, because he's right, we do this all the time. He's saved our asses plenty of times by filling in on the phones before now.

"Back soon."

Caleb strides out ahead of me. As he passes the sofa, he reaches out and pats Angelo's shoulder. Squeezes it, like in comfort.

Angelo's mouth presses in a line.

I don't get it. I don't get *any* of this, but there's someone out there in trouble so the good news is I don't have to. Reading the room—I'm shit at that. But Mountain Rescue? I'm good. *Really* good.

And I have a job to do.

57

9

Katy

The library is spooky at night. Miriam warned me when I offered to stay late, saying I wanted to catch up on re-shelving. The truth is, though, I wanted to clean like a demon. Burn off some of the nervous energy that's been buzzing under my skin since Beau called yesterday about our date.

Italian food. That's what we're getting.

I freaking *love* Italian food.

I'm gonna drop spaghetti in my lap, I know it.

My elbow twinges as I scrub at a mark on the wall—a smear on the white paint where it got dinged by a stray cart. Miriam would kill me if she knew I stayed late for *this*.

Oh well. I needed to do *something*, and my own apartment has been scrubbed until it shines over the last few days. I keep thinking over and over that this is a mistake, that I *just* publicly declared myself dead inside, and now I'm getting tangled up over a date with Beau.

I'm lucky Miriam's a good boss. When I told her about my change of tune, she gave me a knowing smile, but that's all. She didn't say 'I told you so'. She didn't make me feel like more of an idiot than I already do.

"Clean up, you stupid wall." I scrub harder, my hair hanging in my face. I'm red-faced and sweaty, mouth twisted in a grimace, and I jump up with a shriek when I hear his voice.

"Interesting technique."

I fall back against the wall, panting. My heart is pounding so hard, *he* must be able to hear it.

"...Angelo."

He's ten feet away, leaning against the Local History bookcase, a statue in the shadows. Moonlight filters through the closest window, painting him a ghostly silver color and making his white button-down shirt glow.

I find my voice. "The library's closed."

He smiles. The shadows deepen on his face.

"I know. I'm not here for a book, Katy Poole."

"No?" Oh god. My palms are damp.

He shakes his head. "No. I'm here for you."

And—okay. I've heard everyone calling this guy creepy. But I didn't really see it myself, not until now. Not until he cornered me late at night in the silent, shadowed library. Not until he said my full name like that, rolling it around his mouth like he was tasting me.

My cloth lands on the cleaning cart with a soft thump. I cross my arms, so he can't see my fingers trembling.

"Don't be a creep, Angelo."

He chuckles softly. "Not many people say it to my face."

"Well, they should."

"I expect you're right."

My breath catches when he pushes upright. He strolls over to me so slowly, his steps muffled by the carpet, and I press my shoulder blades back into the wall.

I could scream.

I could run.

I could spray him in the eyes with bleach.

"Angelo," I warn.

He stops within an arm's reach.

"Don't be afraid of me, Katy Poole." His soft voice rolls over my skin, soothing my skittering pulse. I melt a fraction, my rigid muscles softening. "I'm curious. That's all."

He's not the only one. Angelo 'Smith' is a walking enigma, somehow brightening up this town and bring a sense of foreboding in one go.

He's like a character from a movie. A villain in one of my books. Magnetic and charming, obviously a bit unhinged, and so freaking *tempting*. Watching him move around the town is like watching a twister tearing down the highway toward you.

"What are you curious about?"

"You. What he sees in you."

Damn it. It's about Beau. It's always about Beau. Disappointment is a heavy lump in my chest, and I give Angelo a sour look.

"Maybe you should ask him."

Angelo hums. It's a low, velvet sound. "But then when he told me, I'd get *ever* so jealous."

I choke back a laugh, even as that disappointment pinches tight. What would it be like to have a man like Angelo obsessed with you? Overwhelming? Maybe. Intoxicating? Definitely.

I bet Beau hasn't even noticed.

It's almost enough to make me feel sorry for Angelo, but then he's stepping forward, crowding me against the wall until there's barely an inch between our bodies. His warmth bleeds through the front of my t-shirt; his clean, expensive scent laces the air; and with every inhale, his chest brushes lightly against mine.

I probably smell like sweat and cleaning products.

I probably look all flushed and sticky.

Angelo doesn't seem to care. He ducks his head, one palm resting lightly on my shoulder as he burrows into the crook of my neck and inhales. My hairs flutter from his breath, traitorous heat pooling between my thighs, and I let out the most humiliating whimper.

His chuckle vibrates into me. The tip of his nose traces up my neck, over my cheek and temple and into my hair. He moves slowly, so slowly, his thumb rubbing gentle circles on my shoulder, and I stand there like an idiot. Frozen in shock and sudden want.

I thought... he was smaller. Most of the time I see him, it's in the distance, and he's with Beau. And Beau would make *anyone* look tiny—he'd give the jolly green giant a Napoleon complex.

But now, when he presses close, his broad shoulders blocking out the moonlit window, completely surrounding me with his body and his warmth...

I know better. Angelo's not small at all.

"Ah, yes." Sharp teeth nip at my earlobe, and I'm winded, scrabbling to grip his sleeves for balance as he keeps talking. "I do see it, actually. Beau has excellent taste."

What does that *mean*? Does he—is he—

"I'm sure you'll both enjoy your date."

Reality crashes back in like one of the mountain's rock slides. I brace my palms against Angelo's chest and shove, but he moves back easily, like he was waiting for the signal. And I hate that, I hate it took me this long to push him off.

"Beau needs better friends." It comes out wobbly, but Angelo nods. He's calm and poised, not at all flustered by what we just did. One palm smooths down the front of his shirt, ironing out imaginary creases.

"Yes. We're in agreement there."

"You don't really care about him, do you?"

For the first time tonight, Angelo scowls. "Wrong, Katy Poole. I would kill for Beau."

Holy crap.

I don't think that's an exaggeration.

Not when Angelo's fingers flex, like some ancient muscle memory, and he turns to stare out the window, a muscle ticking in his jaw. This man is dangerous, and it's not that everyone else in the town is super judgmental. It's that they sense something about him I don't.

Or didn't. I'm reassessing now.

And Angelo is… not right.

"You need to leave." My voice sounds stronger than I feel. I grip the cleaning cart with a sweaty hand, yanking it between us, then snatch up the spray bottle, my finger on the pump. "And don't come back when the library's closed."

"Or what?" He's still staring out the window, voice distant.

"Or I'll spray bleach cleaner in your eye."

That gets a reaction. He jerks around to stare at me, a delighted grin spreading over his face when he sees the spray bottle in my hand. He rocks on his heels, practically bursting with glee, and when he starts backing toward the exit, his words bounce back to me.

"Oh, Katy Poole. How delicious. Perhaps I'll keep you, too."

* * *

My legs wobble all the way home. It's not even that late, barely past 10pm, but getting cornered by Angelo in the library has set me on edge. Made me see this quiet mountain town with fresh eyes. And now every shadow seems too deep, filled with sinister movement; every rustling branch is someone reaching for me from the darkness.

"Damn it, Angelo."

I pick up the pace. My satchel bounces against my hip as I hurry, scurrying down the sidewalk like a mouse running back to its hole.

I'm not *scared* of him. Or okay—maybe I am. But in the sane, reasonable way that a woman is scared of an unhinged man. And if he tries to creep me out again, I'll be ready. I'll kick him in the nuts, not melt against his sculpted chest like a desperate loser.

"Asshole," I grumble, hopping off the sidewalk to cross the street. I hate that he knows I did that. It's not a private, shameful secret—it's something he can use against me. Maybe tell Beau about.

Ugh.

Whatever. I'm a single woman—I can get hot and bothered over a psychopath if I want. Beau needs to date me before he can stake a claim. And now I'm pissed off and flustered for a whole different reason, tangled up in knots, and I could weep with relief when I reach my building, rushing up the stone steps.

I live on the top floor of a townhouse. Okay... it's an attic. But I'm short, so I don't need tall ceilings! And the views of the mountains—they're the real deal. Usually I grumble about all the stairs, but tonight, more than anything, I need to burn off this frazzled energy.

The cleaning didn't help, so I'm still nervous about my date with Beau tomorrow, butterflies flapping in my stomach. But now it's worse, because there are Angelo-nerves there too, and guilt, and horror, and so much unrelieved sexual tension I could scream.

So I pound up those steps like I'm training sprints for the Olympics. And when my thighs burn, going hot and leaden as I climb, I push harder, gritting my teeth, my satchel thumping against my hip.

I shouldn't have done that.

Shouldn't have done *any* of it.

God. I need to tell Beau.

My apartment is shadowed when I burst through the front door, and the first thing I do is charge through all the rooms and flick on every single lamp. It's silly to think Angelo would be here, too—the door was locked, and there's only one key—but I've had enough creepy shadows tonight to last me a lifetime.

Next time I have an evening shift at the library, I'm taking a bunch of night lights and plugging them in around all the walls.

I feel better once it's bright. A bit better, anyway. But I'm still hot and restless, a persistent ache throbbing low in my stomach, and my nerves are sparking under my skin.

There's an obvious answer... but I will *not* get myself off thinking of that man. Nor Beau Walker—not when it was someone else who wound me up so tight. I'm not going there at all, nope, no way, so that leaves stomping into my bedroom and emerging five minutes later in my gym clothes.

Need to burn off these nerves somehow.

So I balance my laptop on the wobbly coffee table. Shove an armchair against the wall. Then work through an hour's worth of YouTube workout videos, praying to any gods that might be listening that Angelo's not watching me right now.

I lunge and squat; I gasp through endless crunches; I hold a trembling, sweaty plank. By the time I'm done, I'm the color of beetroot, my icy blonde hair sticking to my cheeks.

But I feel calmer. My head is clear. And Angelo is back to being a pain in the ass—nothing more.

I'm going to dinner with Beau Walker tomorrow. My heart patters faster at the thought of it, and I gust out a sigh.

There's only one way this love story goes.

And I should know—I'm a librarian.

10

Angelo

Beau picks Katy Poole up from her apartment, stabbing the intercom with one blunt finger then retreating to the sidewalk to peer up at the windows. I wish I could see the exact expression on his face, but my view is obscured by fluttering tree leaves and a bus stop shelter. I'm making do.

He's dressed more smartly than I've ever seen him. He must have ducked into one of the town's few clothing stores while I was playing poker with Caleb in the Mountain Rescue headquarters yesterday. I'd have noticed if he wore a shirt like *that* before—a deep aubergine color, and more fitted than his usual potato sacks.

It emphasizes the swell of his arms.

And his waist tapers in more than I realized.

Shit.

Katy Poole looks good too. She comes hopping down the steps like some fairy princess, and I'd hate her if she didn't look so fucking *cute*. Her pale green dress hugs her curves and flutters around her knees, and her icy hair is wound up in a chignon.

Beau sways back on his heels, like he's been struck dumb.

I know the feeling.

No. No, this is not good. I don't want them smiling shyly at each other—don't want her reaching out, tangling their fingers together. Even from my hiding place, the contrast between them is compelling. Her small hand held by his big, scarred one. Her blonde hair next to his black beard. Outwardly, they're a pair of opposites, but inside…

They're both suckers. Over-romantic saps.

Shit.

I need to fuck this up.

I won't be pushed out. Not even by gorgeous Katy Poole, with her delicious green apple scent and her soft curves. I won't step aside and let them live happily ever after, while I'm tossed out into the cold like some rain-soaked puppy in a cardboard box under a bridge.

No. If Beau doesn't screw this up himself… I'll have to help it along. The thought brings an alien twist to my gut, but I push it away.

Guilt has no use for me now. God knows I've done far worse before, in my old life as my father's loyal soldier. I was *proud* to be a Marino; I took great pleasure in making our enemies despair. My hands are drenched in blood.

This is nothing. A little romantic meddling, nothing more.

They take a winding route to the restaurant, strolling along the sidewalk like lovers in Paris. People stop and stare, nudging each other and whispering together, but either Katy and Beau don't notice or they don't care.

It's always been stupid the way the locals here are scared of Beau—unlike me, he's gentle. There's nothing to fear. So maybe it's good for him to be seen this way—as a normal man on a date. Non-threatening. Desirable.

The restaurant is a green, red and white monstrosity, complete with accordion music drifting out of the open doorway. Candles flicker on the tables through the big glass windows, and the tablecloths are rustic.

I lean against a lamppost across the street, not bothering to hide. Beau and Katy are too wrapped up in each other to notice me, anyway.

He booked a table. I heard him do it three nights ago, his voice grating and awkward on the phone. A server meets them in the doorway, sweeping out an arm and welcoming them inside like a friendly uncle ushering them into a family reunion.

I chew on the inside of my cheek.

I could sneak in, too. Ask for a table nearby—close enough to eavesdrop but not so close they notice me. Force-feed myself some terrible Italian food in the name of snooping. Or I could shuffle around on the street—try and find a good angle to lip read, and count how many times either of them says my name.

She might tell him about the library. About me freaking her out and nibbling her earlobe.

I couldn't help it. Katy Poole is so perfectly plump, like a juicy ripe peach just begging for me to sink my teeth in.

But something tells me Beau won't see it that way.

Better not to lipread, then. Don't want to get my feelings hurt.

Of course, sabotage requires a certain amount of *wading in.* Getting my hands dirty. Outright meddling. And I followed him down the mountain with that precise idea, but now that I'm here, now that I've seen their shy smiles and blushing cheeks—

It bears more thought.

Not tonight. I'll let them have tonight.

Going soft, a voice whispers in my head as I turn on my heel and stride away. It sounds suspiciously like my father's, and I bark a laugh as I picture him here. Seeing his least favorite son—his *rabid dog*—walk away. Allowing them a few hours of happiness, even though it puts my own goals at risk.

He must think I'm dead by now.

I smirk up at the sunset.

* * *

There was a neighbor near Dante's cabin. That's how they escaped me the first time: Dante distracted me with his—his *woman*—and the neighbor came barging through the trees in his truck.

He must have lived close by. Close enough to sneak out for his truck, then rush back and steal my brother away.

So even if Dante's moved on from his cabin...

There's still hope of finding my brother yet.

I don't particularly want to see him. Dante made his choices, and none of them were me, but his turning up at the cookout has forced my hand.

It's cat and mouse. Hunt or be hunted.

And I've got Beau now. I won't let my big brother ruin things.

The handgun nestles neatly in my palm, and I move quietly through the trees. I found Dante's abandoned cabin much quicker tonight, the location seared in my brain. And stalking through the dying light, weaving between shrubs and tree branches, is the perfect distraction from what's happening at that Italian restaurant.

I should have stopped it already: Katy and Beau. It would have been easy.

Why haven't I stopped it?

The first cabin I come to is a bust. It's lit up golden from within, the curtains thrown wide open, and there's a couple in their sixties pottering around a small stove. They have matching steel-gray hair, gnarled hands and stiff backs, and the woman smacks the man's hand as he reaches for the wooden spoon poking out of the pot.

Their bickering floats through an open window, following me as I turn back and try a new direction. God, they made love look tedious.

The second structure I find is ruined. This cabin clearly fought one of the mountain storms and lost—there are holes punched in the walls, and half the roof has caved in. Moss hangs in thick clumps from the window sills, and the windows are missing panes of glass like lost teeth.

Nope. Dante would die on the spot before going in there. He plays the big man, but he really hates spiders.

It's third time lucky. Of course it is. After forty five more minutes of walking, I find it: Dante's neighbor lives a few miles due north from my brother's cabin, and I recognize the truck with a single glance. The vehicle is light blue, and there's even a long scratch and dent on one side still from our little chase down the mountainside. Like it's waving hello.

I squeeze the handgun tighter, rounding the truck on soft feet. Pine needles and bits of twig crunch beneath my steps, but the sound is muffled. Swallowed up by the breeze and the explosive flapping of bird wings.

There—on the driver's side. And in the truck roof. Bullet holes.

Whoopsie.

I mean, he could have fixed it. There's been plenty of time.

But maybe Dante is sentimental, or maybe his neighbor is a slob. Either way, it's all the confirmation I need.

The cabin is lit from the inside too, but unlike the first place, these curtains are drawn. Bright slivers of light spill around the edges of the windows, but I can't see inside.

Not without getting closer.

The deck creaks softly under my weight. I pause, breath held, straining to hear the sounds inside the cabin—the pop and crackle of a fire, the low murmur of voices, a stifled giggle.

There's someone home.

Is Dante in there? The question urges me closer, feet careful as I inch across the deck to the windows. My palm is clammy around my gun, and I flex my fingers one by one as I peer through a crack in the curtains.

The cabin looks warm. Cozy. The furniture is artfully scattered, and a Persian rug covers the floor. That's Dante's touch—he's weak for anything beautiful, anything that makes his cold dead little heart feel alive.

But... maybe his heart's not so dead. Not anymore. Because shapes move in the corner of the room, snagging my attention, and that's *Dante*, that's my big brother kneeling up on the mattress with his hands plunged into a woman's hair. She leans over him from the bed's edge, clutching him back just as tightly as they kiss, and then the neighbor is there too.

Placing a hand on Dante's chest and nudging him back to sprawl on the mattress. Catching his wrists easily and lashing them to the bed frame, Dante's eyes mischievous as he peers up at the other man.

Not just a neighbor, then.

I suspected. But now it's confirmed.

Because who would risk their life for their neighbor, the way

71

these two did? It should have been obvious, especially after they walked into the cookout like that, the three of them practically draped over each other.

They look interesting together—the three of them. I see why Dante likes the arrangement—it's an aesthetically pleasing group of people, worthy of any artwork. The woman's soft curves and dark hair, paired with the man's golden complexion and hard muscles.

And my brother in the middle, sharp-eyed and dark haired and so sly.

The deck groans as I shuffle closer, so close the window fogs from my breath, but they don't even glance up. They're lost together, lost in their own world as the man kisses my brother and the woman straddles his hips. Their muffled laughter seeps through the cabin wall.

I could stay. Watch the evidence of my brother's love, like scrubbing salt in my own wound. My own loneliness.

Or I could go in there. If I want my brother vulnerable, I'll get no better opportunity. His hands are literally tied, he's sex-drunk and hazy, and I have the element of surprise.

My finger flexes against the side of the gun, and I heft it idly. So pleasingly heavy.

But... no. I'm not in the mood. Not to be a voyeur or a killer. And when I step away from the window, the whispering of the trees fading back in, there's a prickle of awareness at the back of my neck. Something nudging for my attention—a thought. An *idea*.

If Dante Marino can take two lovers... why can't I?

Yes, my brother has always seduced easily, attracting anyone who caught his eye. And by comparison, I've scared off more than I can count—with awkwardness as a teenager, then with fear as a man.

The stories about Angelo Marino preceded me.

But it's different now. Beau is not scared of me, and neither is Katy Poole. I unnerve them both, that's probably a fair statement, but she smiled for me. And he built me a room in his cabin.

When I'm with them both, I feel slightly more human. More tethered. Less likely to snap.

And when I think of them settling down without me, my lip curls back from my teeth. *No.* I want to be there too.

So.

It's decided, then.

I'm going to keep them both.

11

Beau

The summer season on Lonely Mountain comes with three things: mosquitoes. Sunburn. And tourists. The town streets suddenly throng with people; the cafes and restaurants open late and throw their doors wide; and at Mountain Rescue, our phone rings off the hook for three months straight.

Usually, I'd pretty much move into the headquarters. Live out of my locker, stopping back at the cabin only to swap out a bag of clothes and sweep away any new cobwebs from the window panes.

But this year, I've got Angelo.

And Katy. Pretty little Katy Poole.

She's not *living* with me obviously—I should be so lucky. A woman like that, I'd roll out the red carpet. I'd build her any room she wanted, just to make her smile.

But it's early days with Katy, so it's just Angelo with me at the cabin. And even though he's been there nearly a full year, I still don't feel right leaving him there all alone every night. It seems rude.

Plus…

Well, I miss the asshole. When the shifts stretch on longer and longer, and we start skipping meals to go out on calls, I find myself talking to him in my head. Telling him about what I'm doing.

It's kind of funny. I'm way chattier with Angelo in my head than I am in real life.

I might feel like an old fool, but I'm pretty sure he misses me too. Over the last two weeks, I've barely stopped back at the cabin in between shifts, and every time I duck through the door, he stares at me with those bright, keen eyes.

The way he looks at me sometimes—it's like he's drilling right down to my marrow. And I feel bad, because every free minute I get these days, I'm spending on Katy Poole.

Walking her home from the library at night.

Taking her to drinks or dinner.

Showing her the best views off the lower peaks—then pinching myself when she reaches up, tugging on my shirt until I lean down and kiss her the way I've been craving, my blood simmering in my veins.

It's… good. Better than good.

It doesn't feel real, it's so bright and light and shiny with her.

But there's something—a niggling voice at the back of my head. I'm missing something. Something important.

"Out again tonight?"

Angelo watches me closely as I stamp my boots on the doormat, kicking off the worst of the mountain debris. He's lounging at the breakfast bar, dressed in a black button down shirt and dress pants. I don't know where the hell he got those—there's no store in our town selling them, that's for sure.

But it's Angelo. I probably don't want to know.

His laptop is levered open on the bar, and as I glance at it, he hits a button to dim the screen. There's no internet in our cabin, but my gut still flips. Angelo could find trouble in a locked, empty room.

"Yeah." After a long stretch of him staring at me expectantly, I remember his question. "I'm taking Katy to a movie."

There's one movie theater in town. It's a relic, all lurid faded carpets and a popcorn machine with a handle, but it's the best I can offer her here. Plus I'd go for any excuse to sit next to Katy Poole in a dark room.

"Lovely." Angelo drums his fingers on the bar, then flips his laptop closed with a snap. "You two are getting along nicely."

"Uh. Yeah."

It's a weird thing for him to say, but honestly, I'm glad to hear someone else say it. It's not as reassuring as if it came directly from Katy, but I figure no one watches me as closely as Angelo. He should know.

The chess board sits empty on the kitchen table, the pieces stashed away in a faded velvet bag. The sight makes my chest pinch—we haven't played in a long time. Weeks, maybe.

Does he miss it too?

"Want to play?" I don't have time, not really, but I'll take my truck down to meet Katy instead of walk. Suddenly, I don't want to leave here tonight without seeing Angelo for a while first.

"Of course." He hops off his stool. "I'm always happy to beat you, Beau."

I snort. Such an asshole.

We fall into an easy rhythm: setting up the board, grabbing two drinks, and settling opposite each other at the table. I take the chance to stare at him more than usual, and I'm not pleased with what I find.

Dark shadows under his eyes.

Hollowed cheeks.

There's something wrong with Angelo.

Whatever it is, it doesn't stop him from kicking my ass. He plays quickly, lounging in his chair and gazing idly around the cabin like he's not even concentrating. And maybe he's not, but my brain doesn't work like his does. Doesn't run at a thousand miles an hour, plotting and scheming and working out plays several turns before they happen.

Angelo huffs as he takes my knight. "You're getting worse. You should practice more."

"I've been busy."

He goes quiet again.

Shit.

We've played in silence plenty of times. More nights than not, we spend hours together in the same room but barely exchange three words. But this is different: this silence is thick. Loaded. And I get that prickling sensation again, like something's happening around me, happening *to* me, and I haven't noticed it yet.

"Angelo?"

"Yes?" He swipes my knight, placing it on the table at his side with a *thump.* His fingers are strong but elegant where they curl around the piece, his nails neater than mine.

I open my mouth, but I don't know what to say. This was stupid.

"Nothing." I take a pawn. "Your move."

One thing I like about playing Angelo is that he's merciless. He never takes pity on me—never makes me feel like a dick by pretending to lose. He beats me every single time, and that's just fine by me. He earns those wins.

This win feels more savage than usual. Like he's not just beating me fair and square—he's toying with me. Dragging it out and making me skip in circles.

"Angelo," I growl after a while.

He smirks. There's some color back in his cheeks.

"Yes, Beau?"

"Stop playing with me."

He pouts. "But you're my favorite toy."

I glare down at the board, my skin flushing hot. My pants are suddenly uncomfortably tight, but I can't fidget in my chair. He'll see, and he'll know what he does to me, and Angelo has more than enough ammunition to use against me already.

He picked out my weak spots within a week of moving in here, even in his painkiller-addled haze. But *he* wasn't a weak spot back then. Not yet.

Katy Poole's sunshine smile flashes across my mind, and guilt curdles in my stomach. It's a familiar sensation—seems like no matter who I spend time with these days, I'm feeling guilty about the other. Missing the person who's not here.

Would Katy laugh at me if I told her that?

Would she think I was crazy? Or—or *wrong?*

"Check mate." Angelo reaches over and flicks my king down. It's rude, I guess, but I always let him surrender for me. It's not like I have any more moves left to offer.

"Well played."

He grunts, sweeping an arm over the board, gathering the pieces back into their bag. And he's already going quiet again, retreating behind a frown, and I can't stand it.

"Come with us."

Two pale eyes land on me like headlights. His hands are still, the chess pieces half packed away.

"Excuse me?"

"Come with us." The words grate out, my throat tight for some reason, but even though I've got a million misgivings about this, I won't take it back. That would be low. "We're going in an hour." I can't help my grin. "You'll like it. It's a mob movie."

He blinks at me, startled, but I don't know why he's surprised. *Angelo Smith.* Please. Did he think I was a complete idiot?

"You want me to come on your date." A smile spreads across his face, slow and languid, and I don't bother to correct him. It's not like I *want* him there.

But I don't want him stewing up here all alone.

And okay... maybe I do want him there. A bit.

* * *

I warn Katy before we head down. Give her a chance to back out, to make an excuse, and who could blame her if she did? I just invited some guy along on our date. But though she's taken aback, her pause echoing down the phone, she doesn't cancel.

"Angelo?" She sounds kind of strangled. "Sure, okay. That sounds... it'll be fun."

"See you soon, Katy Poole," he calls from across the room, shrugging on one of my old jackets. It looks good on him.

She splutters. I scowl.

This is my fault. Whatever insanity Angelo unleashes on Katy now, I brought it on her. I deserve whatever she censure she brings. I'm mulling over that thought, really stewing in my bad decision, when we file out of the cabin and I tug the door shut behind us.

"Wait a second." I glance around from locking the door. Angelo's standing close enough I could count his eyelashes. They're long, so long they're almost feminine, and when he blinks, I can't look away.

"You're on a date, Beau Walker. Not headed for a hoe down."

He tugs at my collar, flipping a stray corner down and smoothing it flat, his palms warm through the thin cotton of my shirt. I stand rigid, waiting for him to be done, trying to commit the sensations to memory.

God, I really am an old fool.

"If you were dating *me*—" I startle, rocking back on my heels. Has he thought of that too? But Angelo carries on, like he's talking about the weather, nothing more. "—I'd take you to bed just to get rid of these ugly clothes. They're an eyesore."

"Good thing I'm dating Katy," I rasp.

"So you are." Angelo winks. "Let's go."

My shoulders prickle where he touched me for the whole drive down the mountain. The skin's heated, oversensitive where it's brushed by my shirt, and I nearly miss the turning for town.

Angelo tuts. "No escape now, Beau."

It's relentless, his teasing, all the way from the cabin until we're stood shoulder to shoulder at Katy's door. She comes down as soon as we buzz, and her smile is jittery as she joins us on the street.

I'm sorry, I want to tell her as I take her hand.

But I'm not sure I am.

Especially when Angelo lopes to her other side, falling into step and asking her about her day. He compliments her dress; he brushes the small of her back as we cross the road.

If she weren't holding my hand, I'd think he was the one dating her.

And Katy's just as startled as I am. Her wide eyes dart to me, checking my reaction, but when I manage a smile she seems to relax. Chats back to him, their conversation more fluid than mine is with either of them.

"You've changed your mind, then?" she asks him at one point, clutching my hand as we weave between tourists along the sidewalk. "About keeping a distance?"

I frown at them both. I don't follow. But apparently neither of them feel like filling me in. Angelo smiles at her, and for once, it's not a smirk. His eyes crinkle at the edges, his whole face warming, and my stomach flips.

"Yes. I found an alternative solution."

"Oh?" She's half laughing. The breeze catches in her sun dress, whipping the white skirt around her thighs.

Angelo's eyes flick down then back up. His voice lowers. "Yes. A perfect solution."

They fall quiet for a moment, and when they start up again, they're talking about the library.

Okay.

So Angelo knows Katy. They seem to have some—some *history*, a shared context. That's fine. It's good, even.

So why do I feel left out suddenly? Or worse—like there's a joke here, and it's on me?

"Turn here," I grind out, steering Katy into the movie theater. If I left them to it, they'd probably sail right past it. She flashes me a smile, walking ahead of me into the vintage lobby, and Angelo steps up to walk at my side.

"What game are you playing?" I speak to him out of the corner of my mouth. His soft laugh makes my jaw clench.

"Relax." His elbow brushes against my side, and again my skin flushes hot. I'm back on the deck again, his face close to mine and his palms on my shoulders. "It's a new game for us. But when we play this game, we *all* win."

12

Katy

D id I want Angelo 'Smith' to crash my date with Beau? No. No, I did not. I figured he was messing with me, trying to find a new way to warn me off. To drive me away.

But even thinking the worst, I still agreed to come. Why? Because I haven't seen Angelo in weeks, and he's been...

Well. He's been on my mind.

He's magnetic. Handsome and sharp and charming, with an edge of danger that makes my blood pump faster.

So I admit it. I wanted to see him. And it turns out, he's not messing with me. Not that I can tell, anyway.

Angelo is acting like a perfect gentleman. Like *he's* the one dating me, and Beau's here like some old-timey chaperone. I'd feel weird about that, but hey—Beau's the one who brought him along.

And it's Beau who leads me into the back row of the theater, brushing imaginary specks of dust off my red cushioned chair before I sit down. He may have rough manners, may speak in grunts half the time, but Beau's a gentleman too.

Angelo settles on my other side. He's not dressed like the other men in this town—he's in a black button down shirt and gray dress pants. He looks more like a city slicker, or like a model who wandered off a runaway. A vision in gray-scale.

He leans close and murmurs: "You're staring at me."

Crap. I whip my head around, looking forward. On my other side, Beau leans in, his beard tickling my cheek, and says: "You okay? Is he freaking you out?"

Yes. Yes, but not in the way Beau thinks. He's making me restless; pushing my buttons like only Angelo can. But I can't say that, and I don't want to lie, so I shrug feebly and stare straight ahead until the screen flickers to life, then act like the commercials for expensive cars and video games are the most fascinating things I've ever seen.

I don't look to either side.

I ignore the warmth coming off their legs, both brushing mine.

And I pretend that their two scents aren't making my head spin. Wood smoke and soap on one side. The faint scent of cologne on the other.

When the movie starts, I sigh with relief, melting back against the velvet padding.

A mob movie. I chuckle quietly, and Beau nudges my arm, grinning at me in the gloom. Maybe we didn't plan for him to come, but it's like our date was already Angelo themed. The figures on the screen are even dressed like him—all sharp suits and sharper smiles.

How does a modern-day mobster end up on Lonely Mountain?

Maybe one day he'll tell us.

My chair creaks as I lean over to Angelo, smoke billowing

and blood spattering on the screen.

"I picture you as more of a vintage mobster. You know, like Al Capone era? Pinstripe suits and those trilby hats. Speakeasies and flappers."

He huffs. "Does *everyone* know?"

"Everyone who's paying attention. What's your real last name?"

"Marino."

Shit.

Everyone knows the Marinos. They're notorious—both for being richer than god, and for the trail of bodies they made on the way to the top.

Angelo Marino...

I need to do some Googling.

"Don't look me up," he says suddenly, like he read my mind. "I don't want you to do that."

"Why not?"

Our heads are close together now, our whispers swallowed up by the explosions on screen.

"Because you're not afraid of me, Katy Poole. I like that. If you look me up, you'll ruin all the fun we have."

"All the more reason to research you."

He grunts, annoyed. "Most of it is not true anyway."

"Really?"

There's a long pause. Bullets pop on screen.

"Half of it is not true. Let's say fifty percent."

"Then why—"

"I was a convenient scapegoat. The Marinos' rabid dog."

"And the half that *is* true?"

Angelo shrugs, his shoulder shifting against mine. And he's completely unapologetic when he says: "I'm better now, Katy

Poole. *So* well behaved."

Maybe we're both crazy, because I believe him. Even in the short time I've known him, Angelo has softened somehow. Smirked more and scowled less. It's Beau's influence, anyone can see that—the steady, stern presence of the older man anchoring him, urging him silently to be better.

And I know it's nonsense. Angelo Marino has never thought twice about me.

But part of me hopes it's down to my influence too.

"I'm still going to look you up."

He reaches up slowly, winding a lock of my hair around his knuckle and tugging. Beau shifts on my other side, but I can't pull away. I can barely breathe.

"You're a bad girl, Katy Poole."

I snort. "No, I'm not." I'm a librarian, for heaven's sake. I do laundry every Wednesday night without fail.

But Angelo leans in until his lips brush the shell of my ear, purring his words with that freaking accent.

"Oh, but I know the truth. You want to be."

* * *

Somehow, I survive two hours sandwiched in the dark between two ridiculously hot men. I barely register what's happening on the screen in front of me—instead I spend the whole time mulling over my favorite things about them.

Beau's gentle power.

Angelo's edge of danger.

Their matching resting bitch face.

The way they seem to orbit around each other, communicating without words. When I was growing up, I always wanted a little brother or sister. Hell, a cousin. Someone to be on the same wavelength with, sharing inside jokes and secret nods.

I never got a sibling, but then here are two men who found that as strangers.

And now I want to wedge myself right in the middle of them.

Sitting in the cinema is like a free sample of that. I get both of their heat, their scent, their attention. Half way through the movie, Beau takes my hand, tangling our fingers together on the arm rest. And though Angelo doesn't take my other hand, he shifts closer, pressing his leg more firmly against mine.

I should probably shove him off. Should be offended or something.

Mostly, though, I'm lighting up inside like a firecracker.

When the credits roll, I come back to earth. I'm dating *one* of these men, not two—and I sure as hell don't deserve Beau Walker if I'm gonna make eyes at his friend. I clear my throat, standing quickly and fishing for my jacket, then snatching it out of Angelo's hands when he holds it up for me.

"Sorry. Thank you."

He raises an eyebrow but says nothing. Goddamn it, he always looks so *knowing*.

"You two want a drink?" Beau's watching me closely too, but there's no censure there. Even seated, he's almost the same height as me.

I want to crawl into his lap and confess everything.

I want him to tell me it'll all be okay.

"A drink." I can't look at Angelo. I won't. "Sure. Yeah, that sounds good."

Beau nods, pleased, and stands before placing his hand against my back and guiding me out of the row.

The cool night air is a relief. So is Angelo's decision to walk next to Beau this time—and I'm intrigued to see him lavish the same flirtatious attention on the other man too. He matches his stride; he walks so close their arms brush together.

Beau doesn't pull away. His cheeks flush dark, and he darts a guilty glance at me.

Oh.

Oh.

My feet stumble on the sidewalk, but Beau catches my elbow quickly. He opens his mouth to say something—to apologize, maybe—but I grab his hand and squeeze.

It's okay. That's what I'm trying to tell him. And I don't have the same pseudo-psychic link with him as Angelo, not yet, but I think he gets it. Beau smiles, relieved.

The bar is busy. Jammed full of tourists and veteran hikers, along with the usual gaggle of artists and musicians drawn to the mountain each year. Me, I'd rather hunt down inspiration on a tropical beach, but what do I know? I'm a librarian, not an artiste.

The chatter of the crowd is loud, a constant buzz, and the heat from all the bodies makes my cheeks flush bright red. Beau grabs us a corner table, pulling out my chair like a perfect, grizzled gentleman before wading back towards the bar. Angelo sits next to me, scanning the crowd with quick, keen eyes, one hand hidden beneath the table.

"Are you packing?" I joke, but he startles slightly and withdraws his hand. Places it face down on the table.

"Of course not."

Crap. I'm on a maybe-three-way-date with a mafioso, and he's acting like the bar might be stormed at any moment. I don't know what's more worrying—this situation, or the pulse of heat it sends to my core. I shift on my seat, squeezing my thighs together, and Angelo smirks at me.

Bad girl, he mouths.

It's easy to see Beau coming. He stands head and shoulders above everyone else in the room, and his beard and scars don't exactly help him blend. He scowls as he nudges through the crowd, but when he places three bottles of beer on the table, he flashes me a quick smile.

"Is he behaving, Katy?"

I press my thighs together harder. "Um. Yeah. Overall."

This—this *noise* rumbles out of Beau's chest, and then I'm not the only one who's hot and bothered. Angelo tenses, his pupils dilating, and the way he looks at Beau Walker... he's like a starving man.

I kick Angelo under the table as I swig from my beer.

He flips me off as Beau peers at us, bemused.

"I'm not sure I like this." Beau points at us both. "I can't keep up with half of this shit. You're both gonna run circles around me."

And there it is. Out in the open.

The three of us. The potential here.

I don't want to ruin what Beau and I have. The few dates we've been on—I've loved every second, and I want this to *go* somewhere. I don't want to give him up.

But even more than that, I don't want to come between these two. Hell, they live together. Beau saved Angelo's life. There's a deep bond here, and I don't want to fray it.

"You'll keep up just fine."

Apparently Angelo doesn't share the same fears. He's smirking, triumphant—like the cat who got two bowls of cream.

"I, um..." I trail off when they both look over. Take a long swig from my beer, praying for them to look away.

Don't know what I was going to say anyway.

But they don't push, thank god, and Beau changes the subject. Asks Angelo something about Mountain Rescue. And I sink back in my chair, stomach churning.

How do people do this? It's hard enough putting yourself out there for one person.

And I'm not like these two.

I'm not brave, and I'm only half crazy.

13

Angelo

There is no room for loose ends in my big love story.
I didn't realize I was in one at first, but now that I
know it, I unfortunately have to deal with my brother.
I'd rather not. If it was only about me, I might risk leaving
Dante alive. Let him be happy with his lovers, provided he
didn't come looking for me again. Call me lazy, call me soppy,
call me a romantic, but I find myself rather tired of bloodshed.

But it's not only about me. Not anymore. For the first time
in my life, I have people to protect—and it's out of choice, not
obligation.

It's a heady feeling. Better than any drug, and I should know.
When I was growing up, I sampled all of my family's wares.

But nothing makes me feel like Katy and Beau. And no one
will take them from me. They're not even fully mine yet, and
the thought makes fury swell in my chest.

They're *mine*. And I'm going to keep them safe.

So, fine. One last kill.

It's not like I'm busy.

I play three nights of poker in a row beforehand as preparation, moving big lump sums to Beau's account just in case. He'll take care of Katy if this goes wrong—even after I inserted myself between them, taking over their date.

When we walked Katy home from the bar four nights ago, he could barely take his eyes off her. And when she kissed me goodnight too—a quick brush of her lips, nothing like the movie kiss she gave him—he didn't scowl. He glowed warm with approval.

So I haven't ruined what they have. Oddly, I'm glad about that. It's very out of character.

"Dante," I murmur as I clean my handgun at the kitchen table. Beau's on shift at Mountain Rescue, so I don't have to hide away. Sunlight filters through the cabin windows, and the gun looks uglier than usual. Out of place. "Why did you have to stay on Lonely Mountain? You stupid fool."

I'm out of practice. Rusty. I can feel it with every doubt tugging at my gut; with the way my finger twitches as I grip the handgun. It feels alien in my hand. A relic from a past life.

Fucking Dante.

He put me in that river. I remind myself of that fact as I let myself out of the cabin, the golden daylight so jarring as it filters through the trees. I should have died from that fall, and for many long weeks afterwards, it *felt* like I did.

My body was ruined. Pulverized by the water.

The only thing that saved me was Beau.

So Dante deserves this. For the river—for leaving me at our father's mercy—for lingering here like a bad memory—for *all* of it.

Yes.

He deserves this.

* * *

Their cabin is empty.

That's fine. I came here in broad daylight for a reason. It's a moment's work to pick the lock, pushing the door open with a gentle shove. I hover on the threshold, ears straining, but there's really no one home.

Oh, Dante. He's become so sloppy.

He should know better.

When I snooped inside his abandoned cabin, it was already a carcass. Cold and empty; ruined and stale. Filled more with animal bones and scraps of fur than signs of my brother.

This is the opposite. Everywhere I look in this cabin, there's Dante.

He's in the fine rugs on the floor. The stack of oil paintings leaning against one wall. The designer scarf looped over a coat hook. Though Dante may have settled on Lonely Mountain, he's always been a creature of luxury.

I can't blame him. I chafe at plaid the same way.

What's stranger to see is the way his things mingle with his lovers'. There's a man's jacket hanging on a peg that is too broad for Dante's shoulders—that must be the neighbor's. And there are signs of a woman here, too—clothes draped over the backs of chairs, a faint floral scent on the air.

Three mugs on the kitchen table, their coffee dregs long gone cold.

But only one big bed.

I cross to the sofa, sinking onto the cushions, and rest the gun on my thigh. From here, a person would have to press their face directly to the windows to see me before entering. Otherwise I'm ready, facing the door with an expression that looks much calmer than I feel.

I don't like seeing the evidence of his domesticity. Not with a gun in my hand.

He comes home later than I expect, when the sun is sinking towards the horizon and the light has turned cold. Where does he go for all that time in the day?

No. No, I don't care.

Their steps creak on the deck outside, three voices murmuring together. There's a burst of feminine laughter, and a key spins in the lock. No faces check the windows first.

See? Sloppy.

"Hello, brother." I smile as Dante freezes in the doorway, what little color there is to his face draining away. "Come inside, please. All of you."

His eyes dart to the side. He's wondering if the other two could run. If they'd make it.

"Don't be stupid, Dante." My words are harsher than planned, my irritation at this whole situation breaking through. He's looking at me like I'm the problem, like I threw *him* into a river. Asshole.

"You couldn't drown, huh?" He leads them inside, sweeping out an arm and tucking the woman behind his back. She peers around his shoulder, eyes wide, and the blond man stands at his side.

Would Beau stand next to me like that?

Doesn't matter. We'll never have to find out.

The woman's whispering something. Dante's nodding slightly, head craned to listen.

"Stop it." The whispering stops. I wave the gun around vaguely. "Do not piss me off. I don't care who I shoot."

It could be a scene taken straight from that stupid mob movie, except there's no heat to my words. I sound *off*, like a wooden actor parroting his lines. And sweat prickles down my spine at the realization that I've miscalculated. I'm not the mad dog anymore. I don't remember how to do this.

Dante's watching me closely. I can practically see the cogs spinning in his head, his lightning-quick calculations floating in the air above him.

God, I wish I could play chess with my brother again. Beau is fun, but I've missed the challenge of Dante.

"Why haven't you gone home?"

I'm the one with the gun. I'm supposed to ask the questions. But I find myself answering him, my face flushing hot.

"Home? To what? Our father's open arms?"

Dante grimaces. Yes, he knows where he left me. And for the first time, his gaze rakes over me with something more than cold calculation. With concern. Like he *cares.*

I need to do this fast. Before I lose my nerve.

But—"Beau Walker doesn't like guns." Her voice pipes up from behind my brother's back, and I glare at his chest like I could bore straight through to her.

I flex my grip on the handgun. "How do you know Beau?"

"I see him in the library sometimes." A pile of worn paperbacks snags my eye from the bedside table. And fuck—she might know Katy Poole from there too. They might—they might *like* each other—

A headache throbs behind my temple. I dig at it with the palm of my free hand.

"You are making this very difficult."

Her huff makes Dante's mouth twitch. *"Good,* you psychopath."

No. No, they're relaxing. The blond man is scanning the

cabin, his shoulders still tense, but Dante and the woman are whispering again. My brother's posture has softened. I'm losing control of this room, and that means it won't be my brother lying in the cold ground by nightfall.

I should have left Beau a note.

"Why couldn't you—why couldn't you just *go?*" I rub harder at my temple. The headache is spreading, making my teeth ache. "You already had those two. Why couldn't you let me have this?"

"Have what?" Dante asks quietly. But it's the other man who replies, watching me with something approaching pity.

"Beau Walker."

And Katy Poole. I want to add her name too, but I'd never risk her like that. But let the record show: *And Katy Poole.*

The silence is thick. My hand is clammy around the gun. I adjust my grip.

"Angelo."

I haven't heard my brother say my name for so long. I half wondered whether he'd forgotten it.

"*Angelo.*"

I lower the gun.

Dante's lover is right. Beau wouldn't like this. I knew that when I came here, but I thought it would be quick. Simple. Like pinching off a flower bud, not this disaster. And now I can't stop picturing his face—Katy's too—when they hear what I've done.

My heart beats too slowly as I stare at the nearest rug. It's faded blue, intricately patterned, and I swallow back queasiness as I wait for my brother to finish this.

The floorboards creak. Someone's shifting their weight.

"It's a big mountain, Angelo," Dante says at last.

My neck twinges as I glance up, heart thudding faster now. Dante frowns at me, but there's something else there too. Something hopeful.

I lick my lips. "Perhaps, if you stayed on your patch..."

He nods once, sharp. We're Marinos. We know all about keeping to your territory.

All three of them stiffen when I push to my feet. But I flick the safety on, tucking the handgun back in my waistband.

"I apologize for breaking in."

Dante huffs a laugh. "It's no problem."

"And for pointing a gun at you."

"It was just like old times."

I hover for a long moment, but eventually they realize they're blocking the door. They stumble out of the way, the blond man still tugging the woman behind his broad body.

He's cautious. I can't blame him for that. But Dante's *lack* of caution—that makes my chest sing. My earlier headache is a thing of the past, and I've never felt more clear-headed. Never felt lighter.

Dante lingers by the door. And as I pass him, he claps me on the shoulder and squeezes.

"Maybe, on neutral ground..." he trails off.

"Yes. Maybe."

That's quite enough progress for now.

It's getting dark when I walk down the cabin steps. Twigs crunch underfoot and I set off into the trees, three pairs of eyes boring into my back.

I tense, but the bullet never comes.

Dante's gone soft too.

14

Beau

The second Angelo walks through the cabin door, I stop pacing. "Where have you been—is that a *gun*?"

He pulls the weapon from behind his back, tossing it onto the nearest armchair like he's throwing his keys in a bowl. Everything about his air is casual—everything except for the manic glint in his eyes.

"Yes. I went to kill my brother." I splutter, but he keeps talking, his words tripping over themselves. "I didn't, though. I didn't think you would approve."

"I *don't*."

Angelo rakes a hand through his dark hair, rucking it up at the back as he rounds the armchair, then shoots me a grin over his shoulder as he strides past into the kitchen. "I know. So I changed my mind."

"That's not…" I trail off. I can't finish what I was going to say: *that's not romantic.* Because he looks so pleased with himself, smug and elated, like he's passed some mystic test rather than freaked me out and brought a gun into my cabin.

It reminds me of when I took a stray cat in once. The little asshole used to bring me dead mice, dropping them on my bed and then purring up at me like I should be grateful.

"Angelo."

"Hm?" His voice echoes back from the kitchen. The refrigerator door rattles as he tugs it open, and the weak electric light shines onto the opposite wall. I stand rooted as he rummages through the jars and tubs of leftovers, muttering to himself.

"What?" I call at last when I find my voice. "Almost murdering someone got you hungry?"

"Yes, actually." The refrigerator door slams and he emerges, leaning in the kitchen doorway. He wore one of *my* shirts on his maybe-murder spree. It's dark blue and rolled to his elbows, showing off his toned forearms, and he smirks at me as he licks peanut butter off his thumb. "It's the adrenaline, you know."

"I'm getting rid of that gun."

"If it makes you happy."

"And don't wear my shirts anymore."

He scoffs. "That *won't* make you happy, Beau Walker."

Fuck. No, it won't. He knows I like the sight of him in my clothes, the asshole—that's why he's constantly stealing from my closet. There's no other reason that I—hate—flannel—Angelo would deign to wear so much plaid. He's toying with me.

"Why the hell did you—"

"To keep you safe," he says shortly. I blink at him, lost for words. It's a familiar feeling around Angelo. "You and Katy. But there's no danger—not to you. My brother has lovers too. It's a case of mutually assured destruction."

Lovers.

Heat roars over my face at that word. I can *feel* the flush prickling over my skin, hot enough to cook an egg on my forehead. None of us have stated it so baldly, but of course Angelo wouldn't care. He doesn't have an inch of shame in his body.

His long, toned body, currently wrapped in my shirt and leaning against my kitchen doorway.

Fuck.

"Ah," he murmurs. "You've short-circuited. Shall I pass you a beer?"

I scrub a palm down my face. "No. No, better not."

I want to be sober for this. We all need clear heads. If we're going to do this... we're doing it right. I didn't read half the library's romance section to screw this up now.

For all Angelo's bluster, his eyes widen when I stride up to him. I cup his face roughly, nothing at all like the way I touch Katy. With her, I'm reverent. With *him*... he can take it. He likes it, too.

Angelo's tongue darts out, wetting his bottom lip. His hands snake out, grabbing fistfuls of my shirt at my waist.

The kiss is... gentler than I expect. More tentative. Like he's unsure, like he hasn't had much practice. But that seems ridiculous—the man just tossed a gun on my chair—and yet when I nip at his bottom lip, he groans.

Angelo parts his lips eagerly, lets my tongue sweep into his mouth, and yanks on my shirt, grinding our hips together. He's as hard as I am, hot and rigid through our jeans, and I thrust him back against the door frame.

So, okay—he may be a bit out of practice. Who isn't? He's also hungry, biting, *snarling* into my mouth, and fuck—

I'm ready to burst into flames.

I tear my mouth away while I still have brain cells left. Rest my forehead against his, breathing hard.

"We can't do this." He stiffens then begins to pull away, eyes shuttering, so I shake him. His head bounces softly off the wood. "Don't be an idiot. I mean we can't do this without Katy."

He hums, happy again. His moods are always like this: lightning-quick to change. Like the weather swirling around the mountain.

"I did picture her here."

"So did I."

"Where is she?"

I pretend to think about it. Like I don't know her schedule off by heart.

"She's working late. Closing the library tonight."

The smile that spreads over Angelo's face is pure evil.

"Perfect."

* * *

I've never snuck up on a person. It seems a weird thing to point out, but Angelo clearly has a ton of practice. He melts into the shadows as we stroll down the town sidewalks, like it's automatic. Like he can't help being a bit of a creep.

"Stop that."

He steps back into the moonlight.

"Sorry. Force of habit."

"It's Katy. Don't creep up on Katy."

He smiles to himself, footsteps light and hands shoved in his pockets. "She didn't mind last time."

"What? You stalked h—never mind."

I cut myself off, because you know what? I don't want to know. They've clearly worked it out between themselves, and whatever antics they get up to together, that's their business.

But *I'm* not going to sneak up on a woman in the dark, and I tell him so.

"Oh, go on." His teeth glitter in the moonlight. "You should at least try it once. Live a little, Beau."

"No."

"There's a difference between psychotic creeping to murder someone and romantic creeping for her pleasure. I should know."

There's so much to unpack in that sentence. I'm not equipped. So I huff and shake my head, making sure my boots thump loudly against the sidewalk.

"Katy liked it," he murmurs. "Her cheeks went bright pink."

I sigh. And try to walk softer. I love it when she goes pink.

The library windows glow yellow, casting big pools of light across the town square. We both fall silent as we approach and Angelo slips ahead, guiding me around the edges of the square, keeping to the thickest shadows. I follow, a frown etched on my forehead and my heart pounding against my ribs.

The second I think Katy is unhappy, I'm stopping this.

But first... I want to see if he's right. If she likes a pinch of fear.

There's no one else in the library. Angelo checks first, peering through the windows and humming under his breath. I've never seen him happier, so relaxed and excited. He's visibly turned on, his hard length jutting against his fly.

I force my eyes away. This is about Katy now. I can't get caught up thinking about pushing Angelo against the brick wall, thinking about palming his cock and making him groan again—one of us needs to concentrate. Needs to be normal.

"She's in the stacks." Angelo stares through the window like he's hypnotized. How did I not see that he liked her? I've only ever seen that level of obsession on his face once before, and that's directed at *me.* "Fuck. She looks so cute with that dorky lanyard."

"If we make her uncomfortable—"

"We won't." Angelo's fingertip scratches against the brick. "Katy Poole is a secret bad girl."

I don't know about that, but I sure as hell want to find out. Every date we've gone on so far has been tame—romantic, yes, the best times I've ever had, but still careful. We've been treating each other with kid gloves.

I couldn't shake the feeling that if I was too forward, if I showed her how goddamn primal she makes me feel, then I'd freak her out. That she'd look at me as the town Bigfoot, same as everyone else.

Maybe Angelo's brand of crazy is exactly what we need.

After all—we're sure both drawn to *him.*

"Wait." Angelo goes to step away from the window, and I place a hand on the back of his neck. Not squeezing, not threatening. Just letting him feel the weight of it. A long breath shudders out of him, and I swear he melts back into my touch. "Say the words, Angelo. If she doesn't like it…"

He huffs a laugh, but it's strained. "If she doesn't like it, we'll stop."

I nod, even though he can't see me. "Good."

And I do trust him. I do. But I feel better hearing him say it, knowing that we've drawn this clear line. Maybe this is what I bring to the table—shaving off Angelo's sharp edges. Letting Katy enjoy him without fear.

He opens the door silently. Pulling it slowly, coaxing the hinges not to creak, glancing back at me with a wink. Angelo raises an elegant finger, presses it against his lips, then slips

inside the library.
    I follow.

15

Katy

I slide another hardback onto the shelf, my movements robotic as my mind wanders. I've done this thousands of times before. I only need half my brain to re-shelve all the books and close the library—the rest of me can think about whatever I like.

It used to be that I'd put on a podcast while I worked late. No one ever comes in after dark, so I'd put on a gory true crime show to creep myself out, nerves skittering at the crazy stories. People are a *nightmare*. A complete horror show. And there's no better time to listen to that stuff than when you're in a shadowy, empty building all alone.

What can I say? I like the adrenaline.

Plus nothing ever actually happens on Lonely Mountain. Storms? Sure. Hiking accidents? You bet. But human drama? Hell no. The closest we get is the new throuples scandalizing the old folks.

That could be us.

Beau and Angelo and I.

I bite the inside of my cheek, hiding a smile even though no one's here.

Of course, I'm not gonna get my hopes up. How many men actually want to share a woman? I know they're into each other too, but still. They could change their minds at any time.

Or worse—they might figure out that they just want each other. That I'm extra baggage, getting in the way. They live together, after all, they have way more history together than I have with either of them. On any given night, they might decide to take things further up in that cabin, then decide they don't want to screw it up by adding me.

My stomach twists at that thought. The two of them together up there, tucked away on the mountainside, laughing and kissing and *forgetting* me, and—

A sharp *crack* makes me jump. It echoes across the library: the undeniable sound of a book hitting the floor.

I stand frozen, my breaths coming in short pants.

I'm alone.

I'm alone.

It's okay.

But my heart pounds as I walk slowly through the stacks, scanning the shadows at the edge of the room. My reflection stares back at me, wide-eyed in the glass windows. My blonde ponytail, wisps breaking free around my hairline. My white t-shirt and blue jeans.

Stupid podcasts. They've ruined me for the late shift. If Miriam could see me spooked like this, she'd laugh her ass off. I'd never hear the end of it.

A door clicks shut on the other side of the room.

Oh my god. Oh my god. I spin around, snatching a heavy textbook off nearest shelf. Raising it over my head like a weapon.

"Hello, darling."

…Freaking *Angelo*.

I lower the textbook slowly, still tempted to whack him with it. He lounges at the end of my stack, dressed in one of Beau's blue shirts and dark jeans. He's grinning, eyes sparking with mischief, and rare spots of color glow high on his cheeks.

He freaking loves sneaking up on me.

Asshole.

"Did we scare you?"

"…We?"

The floor creaks behind me. I whirl around, my lanyard flapping against my chest, and find Beau Walker stood at the end of the stacks, his bulk filling the space between the shelves.

He's a big guy, Beau. And with his beard and his scars and his default scowl, it would be so easy to be frightened of him.

If you didn't know him, anyway.

"Thank god." Beau smiles faintly as I blow out a relieved breath. I jab a thumb over my shoulder. "I thought he'd finally snapped."

Beau's chest rumbles. "I'd protect you, Katy."

"But that's not what she *wants*." Angelo sounds irritated now, his words clipped, and Beau watches the other man closely as he steps up to my back. Angelo's palms skim up my arms, not quite touching me, the heat making my skin prickle.

I'm alone in the library at night. Alone with two men. Two men who snuck up on me, and one of them is *touching* me, and…

My breath hitches.

Beau's eyebrow quirks.

"See?" Angelo buries his nose in my hair and sniffs. Inhales my scent like a predator. "You should see some of the stuff she reads, Beau. It would make your eyes water."

"*Asshole*." I throw my elbow back without thinking, but Angelo dodges easily. He's still at my back, still surrounding me with his warmth and his scent and his toned arms. "You can't pretend to be all insightful and all-knowing if you're just snooping through my eReader."

Beau chuckles, taking one step closer. His hands are in his pockets, his posture casual, but I know him. I see the tension running through his shoulders.

Angelo nips my earlobe. "Sure I can."

His breath is warm against my neck, and I twist in his grip. Not fighting him, not really, but feeling him everywhere. Relishing it. He's hard, his length digging into my back, and I squirm against it, making him choke out a laugh.

"You two have a little book club going on. I wanted in on that action."

"It's not a club if you're the only one who knows about it." Crap, I sound so breathless.

"Huh." He slides a hand into my hair, tugging out my hair band and flicking it onto the carpet. Beau grunts, annoyed, and bends down to pick it up. He holds it up for me then changes his mind and tucks it into his pocket. "Alright. Katy Poole, I'm reading your books. *All* of them. Even the ones that come with warnings. Even the ones that have been *banned*, you dirty girl—"

I throw my elbow back again but Angelo dances out of the way, then bands his arms across my front and crushes me against his chest. He may not be Beau-sized, but he's well-muscled. Strong.

"Wait." Beau's command is deep. Angelo stills. And with all of us frozen, I can feel every pulse of my heartbeat between my legs. Can feel every heightened nerve ending, sparking where my clothes touch my skin.

Beau's steps are heavy. He comes right up to us, not stopping until the toes of his boots nudge my ballet flats and his chest brushes mine with every heaved breath.

A big, warm palm cups the side of my face. A callused thumb traces the edge of my mouth.

"Is he right, Katy? Is this what you want?"

Is this what I want? I've never admitted it to anyone before—not even myself. But I'm safe with these men—I know that deep in my bones. Not just physically, but with my darkest secrets. My desires.

There's no room for shame between us three.

"Um. Yes." I swallow hard and meet Beau's eyes. Angelo's heartbeat pounds against my shoulder blades. "Not in real life, obviously. But as a—a game. With you two. Yes."

Angelo hisses in triumph, and Beau's eyes darken. That's all the warning I get, then Beau's hand joins Angelo's in my hair, grabbing a fistful and tugging my head to the side. It's perfectly judged—forceful, strong, but with only the tiniest sting. I guess big Beau Walker has been walking this line, managing his strength, his whole life.

Maybe one day we'll snap his careful control. Angelo and I, together.

I can't wait.

The scrape of Beau's teeth against my throat makes me groan. I push back against Angelo, needing to feel him too, and his breaths rasp in my ear. Beau's tongue darts out, tasting me, licking a hungry stripe up my neck.

"Oh my god."

I'm burning up, heat crackling through my whole body

like the wildfires that sear the mountains in the summertime. My head spins from the sensations, the two of them so overwhelming, and I sway in their grip, buffeted between two hard chests.

Angelo's hand squeezes my waist.

"Ready, Katy Poole?"

A breathless laugh bursts out of me. "Hell yes."

* * *

We may be new to this, the three of us, but somehow... it's instinctual.

Not flawless. There are a couple of knocked heads. Some fumbles and muffled laughter. But even when our movements are stilted, we're humming along on the same wavelength. Blissfully, beautifully in tune.

Beau slips automatically into command. Ordering Angelo in low, clipped tones, and I don't know why I'm surprised at first that Angelo clearly likes it. He follows each command to the letter, his heart thumping faster against my back, and his rigid cock digs into the base of my spine.

It makes sense. Beau has been *handling* Angelo all year. No one else could have kept him in line, could have curbed his worst impulses and sanded off his sharp edges.

Only Beau.

And something tells me that anyone else trying to boss Angelo around would have a terrible wake up call. Maybe even a sharp blade between the ribs.

Except me, obviously. Somehow I'm his exception too.

"Undo her button." Beau scowls down at my jeans as Angelo flicks them open. He waits to be told before he tugs the zip down. And Beau likes that too, I can tell. His eyes are bright, his pupils blown wide. And his mouth curls with satisfaction every time Angelo obeys, every time the two of us dance to his tune.

"Don't touch her there yet." Angelo's hand stills on its path down my stomach. Cool air wafts against the sliver of my bared underwear, and I whimper, still squirming. I won't stand still for them. Because this is part of it—I want to fight against Angelo's grip, want to ignore Beau's commands. Want to make it hard for them.

All part of the game.

"Hold up her arms."

Angelo grips my wrists and raises them over my head. He pulls them high, so high I'm lifted onto my toes, and I snarl, kicking back at his shins. Beau pinches the hem of my t-shirt and pauses, watching me closely, a muscle ticking in his jaw.

Always so freaking careful, even now. Even with his pupils blown so wide his eyes are nearly black.

"Do it," I gasp, and then my t-shirt is tugged roughly over my head. It catches on my chin, messes my hair, and I'd burst out laughing if I wasn't so turned on. If my racing heart wasn't lodged somewhere in the base of my throat.

Angelo lets go of my wrists long enough to get my t-shirt off. I rock back onto my heels.

"It's warm," he mutters, holding it out to Beau, but I'm already gone. Bursting into a sprint, dashing for the end of the stacks, curses breaking out behind me. I misjudge the corner, my limbs clumsy from everything we've been doing, and my shoulder barges a shelf.

Books slam onto the carpet.

My reflection races past the dark windows, wild hair streaming. My top half bare except for my plain white bra.

It's crazy. This whole thing is crazy, and reckless, and so freaking fun, and when I round a stack and slam into Beau's chest, his arms lifting me clean off the ground, my scream trails off into laughter. He's grinning too, but it's savage, so *feral*, and this is what Angelo does to us. What he brings out of us.

I love it.

The other man doesn't keep away for long. It's not in Angelo's nature to take a back seat, to play third wheel, so I'm not surprised when he tugs me from Beau's grip, crushing me back against his chest like that's where I belong.

"You shouldn't have run, Katy Poole." His teeth scrape over my cheekbone, his hands roaming *everywhere.* The fresh scent of his cologne fills my nose. "It'll be so much worse for you now."

I hiccup a laugh. "Promises, promises."

He's still standing behind me when his lips meet mine. Angelo kisses me hungrily, roughly, craning his neck to reach me at first then stepping around me, never breaking contact. I've thought about kissing him so many times, but I could never have predicted how off-kilter he seems. How uncalculated, for once.

Angelo slants his head, kissing me harder. I suck on his tongue.

He growls.

Beau's hand lands heavy on my shoulder. He spins me easily, pushing me against a bookshelf, then kicks my feet wide.

Oh. My. God.

"Take off her bra."

Angelo's fingers are deft. He flicks the clasp open, then shoves the straps down my arms.

Their low groans echo through the library. I hide my smile behind my hair.

Two sets of hands. One big and rough, one elegant and sure, roaming freely over my bare skin. Scorching trails along my arms, around my stomach, cupping and kneading my breasts. It feels so good that I forget to fight, bracing myself against the bookshelf and holding still while they touch every inch.

Someone pinches my nipples. I'm not sure who.

Something twists deep in my core.

I could weep with relief when blunt fingertips finally nudge inside my underwear. My legs spread wider, my hips pushing back like an offering, and Angelo chuckles darkly in my ear.

"You're perfect like this, Katy Poole." His words are quiet, just for us two. "You both are. Like you're made for me."

I could say the same thing, but my brain can't form words. Not when those fingertips find my clit, glancing over the bundle of nerves, then dipping down to my core. It must be Beau touching me there, because it's his ragged groan when he finds how slick I am. How ready. He gathers my wetness, circling back up to my clit, and then all I can do is hang my head and try to remember to breathe.

Angelo rocks against my ass, still so hard and thick.

What the hell have I gotten myself in to?

Whatever it is, I can't stop. Not even if lightning strikes the library. Because Beau's sliding a finger inside me, and he's so big that even a single finger is a stretch. He pumps it in and out slowly, rubbing my clit with his thumb, and Angelo pinches my nipples again, and the orgasm crashes into me like a landslide. When I come apart...

I *yelp*.

I'd be embarrassed, but I don't have time. Because I'm still settling back into my body, my brain coming back online, as Angelo tugs my jeans and panties down to my knees. There's a crinkle of a foil wrapper, and then the broad head of his cock nudges at my entrance.

"Wait." We both still, frozen in agonizing limbo, panting in the silent library. Angelo's forehead drops to the back of my head, his curse quiet. But Beau turns my chin to face him, his dark eyes clear. "Do you want to keep going, Katy?"

My nod is desperate. So urgent my teeth clack together. And Beau smiles, relief coasting over his scarred face, then ducks his head and kisses me hard as Angelo slides inside me from behind. Beau strokes his tongue into my mouth in the same rhythm, and all the air empties out of my lungs.

Holy shit.

They're *everywhere*. Their scent, their heat, their ragged breaths. Their hard bodies and their grasping hands. Angelo rocks into me, pushing deep with a guttural groan, and Beau's kissing me like he wants to devour me whole. It's better than I ever thought it could be, *sharper* somehow, more overwhelming, more wild.

The heat builds in my core, the tension twisting tighter.

With every rock of Angelo's hips, every nip of Beau's teeth, they lay a claim on me. Declare silently that I'm theirs. And I'll pay them back soon with raking fingernails and bruises sucked onto their collarbones, but right now—

"Oh. Oh, *shit*."

"Come for us, Katy Poole." Angelo's voice is rougher than I've ever heard it. Like it's scraped from the bottom of his chest. He picks up the pace, fucking me harder, faster. "Do it. I want to feel it."

Beau rests his forehead against mine. And his thumb pressing against my lip—it's so *tender.*

I come slower this time. It builds from somewhere deeper, then ripples through me in waves. And Beau watches like he's entranced, while Angelo curses loudly behind me, and it's perfect.

Perfect.

Afterwards, I slump against the bookshelves. Beau moves forward, but it's Angelo who pulls up my jeans. Buttons me up, fetches my t-shirt, and fixes my clothes, even tucking my hair behind my ear.

I stare at him like he's a stranger.

But he's not. Neither of us should be surprised.

Angelo rolls his eyes once he's done, tugging his shirtsleeve straight. "I will pretend not to see your ridiculous shocked expressions. You two have such little faith in me."

"That's not—" Beau begins, but the other man is already dropping to his knees. Tugging Beau's belt open with a determined expression. Next time, I'd like to help, but I'm still too dazed, too clumsy, and honestly—the view is too good from here.

"Tell me no, Beau Walker." Angelo scowls at the button of Beau's jeans.

Beau shrugs, helpless, his eyes darting to me. "I'm not going to do that."

"Then tell me *yes.*"

Beau cups the back of Angelo's dark head. "I... yes."

I offer him a smile as Angelo tugs his jeans open. And Beau nods, his relief and his nerves clear on his face, as Angelo pulls out his cock.

Um... wow.

Angelo snorts, and glances at me over his shoulder. "You got off easy, Katy Poole. Next time."

"Sure," I manage. "Next time."

Beau's rolling his eyes, a dark flush creeping over his cheeks. Because Beau Walker is *proportional.* Even in Angelo's big hands he looks huge, dark against Angelo's pale skin, and I can't look away.

Angelo's thumb rubs over the head.

Beau hisses between his teeth.

I could watch them for hours. Especially when Angelo leans forward, licking a stripe up the base of Beau's cock, then sucks him into his mouth. His cheeks hollow, his eyelids fluttering, and Beau's hand tightens in his dark hair.

But *hours* isn't really on the table. Not after all this freaking build up.

"I can't believe you two never did this before."

Beau told me when I asked. So sue me. I'm nosy.

"Tell me about it," Angelo pulls off to mutter before diving back down. Beau chokes out a laugh.

I lean back against the bookshelves, watching them together, listening to their soft murmurs. Feeling the tiny shock waves still rippling through my body. The library is silent, empty and eerie, and normally around this time, I'd be giving myself a pep talk. Working up the courage to walk home in the dark.

No need for that tonight.

Something tells me I'm not walking home alone.

16

Angelo

Six months later

It was a stroke of genius. More so than usual, even, and that's saying something. I have so many excellent ideas.

Katy and Beau are both romantics. They read all those books together—not Katy's fun ones that *I* reenact with her, but the ones that are sugar-sweet and end with weddings and babies.

I don't know about babies. That seems… well. Insane, even for me. We'd have to think about that. But a *wedding*—that's achievable. We're committed to each other. Woven tight.

Not a traditional wedding, obviously. Not with three of us. And I know it doesn't bother them, not really, but I don't want them to miss out at all. So I made a plan, played five straight nights of poker, and saved up some bribes.

"You know this isn't legally binding, right?"

Caleb hovers on the library steps, tugging at his suit jacket. He's more comfortable in corduroy, the animal. A few feet away in the town square, his two partners are huddled together against the cold, giggling.

The woman, Bianca, has a formal dress under her coat, and snow boots on her feet.

She's a good match for Caleb. I roll my eyes.

"Of all my crimes, this is the least of my worries."

"I'm not saying it's a *crime—*"

The door opens behind him. Miriam pokes her head through the gap, searching for me before she gives a wry smile. "We're ready. Let's get this show on the road. I want to reopen the library to the public."

"No one in this godforsaken town can read anyway." I sail past her, throwing her a wink.

Miriam shoves my shoulder. The cheeky old bat.

It's a small audience, and the rows of chairs fill up quickly. Beau's already at the front, looking so nervous he might throw up. I push past a dawdling friend of Katy's and stride to the front, stopping at his shoulder.

"A suit, Beau Walker? Alert the presses."

A shaking hand smooths down his front. "Angelo. Shut up."

This is the gratitude I get. Typical.

It may be a long time since my life with the Marinos, but I can't help scanning the chairs, then the groups gathered in the stacks behind, searching for familiar faces. Old threats. And I startle at the sight of my brother, standing in between Roxy and Alec. I've met his partners twice, now. Only that one time involved a gun.

Dante nods, his face unreadable but his shoulders relaxed.

I smirk back.

Progress.

Much as she irritates me, Miriam has done well with the library. There are strings lights draped everywhere over the stacks—we had quite the heated debate about candles—and soft string music plays in the background. The overhead lights are dimmed, the chairs draped in soft white fabric, and everyone in here made at least half an effort to look the part.

It's not the extravagant show of wealth and finery it would have been in my previous life. But it will do fine.

Katy looks the best, of course. When she emerges from between the stacks, walking down the aisle in a simple white lace dress, soft murmurs echo through the room. Beside me, Beau is awestruck. And she's smiling so wide, her eyes so bright, that I know I guessed right about a wedding.

A stroke of genius.

When the three of us stand together, listening to my bribed official drone on, I lean down and whisper in her ear.

"Not my favorite role play of ours. But definitely top five."

Her elbow digs into my side.

"It's not a role play, asshole." She mutters out of the corner of her mouth, her smile fixed for the audience. "After today, you're *mine*."

"So territorial," I murmur. But I already knew that. All three of us are fairly primal.

There's no need for adorable threats, though.

I've been theirs for a long time.

* * *

Thanks for reading Their Mountain Bride! I love an unhinged hero, I can't help it. I hope you loved Angelo and his throuple too.

For more group-HEAs, check out the Year of the Harem books!

119

Because when there are so many hot heroes... why choose?

Kayla x

Teaser: Autumn Tricksters

I step one foot back in the carnival and thank God I'm home. Three weeks in Ohio with my straight-laced family was a nightmare. I haven't breathed right since I left this place, since I heard the shriek of the crowd, the roar of flames, the pounding of drums. The scent of popcorn and roasting nuts floats to me on the breeze, and my stomach rumbles.

Finally. It's been three weeks too long.

I nod to the men and women running the stalls. There are shooting games, with the *plink* of air rifle pellets and the clatter of cans dropping to the ground. There are drinks stalls, with fresh roasting coffee and beer on tap. There are tents with fortune tellers; mimes with painted faces, striding through the crowd on stilts; pink vats of cotton candy.

It's a wonderland. An eerie, feral wonderland, where you're just as likely to have your pocket picked as your fortune told.

No sticky fingers come near my pockets. I'm one of these people, and they know better than to go for their own.

I hitch my duffel bag up on my shoulder and weave my way across the carnival grounds. The drink is flowing tonight; the townies getting messy and loud. They shove each other and cackle, their inhibitions slipping away in the carnival's haze. I skip around them, no one coming within an inch of my skin.

Sure, I could stamp my steel-toed boots and barge my way through. But I've had an eight-hour journey with a caffeine headache and a throbbing wrist. I know when to pick my battles. So I duck and weave my way through the crowd, like they're rocks and I'm water flowing around them.

"Hazel!" An older woman running one of the food stalls yells and waves her entire arm. I grin and cut over to her, sniffing at the hot dogs grilling on her cart.

"Hey, Ginny."

I drop my duffel at the base of her stand. Two soft, plump arms wrap around me and pull me close, and I pat her back awkwardly with my cast. When I pull away, one of her long grey hairs sticks to my tongue. I spit it out, grimacing at her roar of laughter.

"You've been away too long, girl."

"Tell me about it."

If I'd had my way, I'd never have left at all. Not even after everything that happened. This is my home.

"Robbie gave you the green light to come back?"

I shrug. "Something like that."

Ginny slices a bun as she talks, her hand deft with the knife. Ginny may look like a sweet old grandma, with her salt and pepper hair and flowery smock dresses, but she can gut a troublemaker quicker than a fish.

The truth is, I never asked for permission to come back. I should never have let them send me away in the first place. If I hadn't been so messed up—freaking out over my busted wrist, heart cracked open by my asshole ex—I'd have stood my ground. Insisted on staying here and resting up in my trailer.

Being home did nothing for me. I didn't get to laze around and eat my Mom's treats, or whatever Robbie expected. I got lectures and disappointed sighs. Pointed looks at my tattoos, my purple hair. A couple of nights, a bible was left pointedly on my bedside table. I came away with raised blood pressure and my fill of fucking cornfields.

Yeah. That was no healing retreat. If Robbie wants to send me away to lick my wounds, next time he can shell out for a spa.

Ginny pushes a steaming hot dog into my good hand, loaded up with crispy fried onions. I groan and snatch up the mustard and ketchup, lashing them on top.

"You're a goddess. A fucking deity." I take a bite and my eyes practically cross.

Ginny laughs and slaps me hard on the back, hard enough that greasy onions shower onto my boots.

"Get gone before Robbie sees you. I ain't wading into that."

It's more than fair, so I balance my hot dog on my cast and swing my duffel back onto my shoulder. Robbie will ream me out when he sees I'm here, and there's no call to drag Ginny into that. Robbie may be young, may be quiet and watchful, but he runs this whole show. When he says jump, we ask how high.

Apart from me, I guess. Just this one time.

I take another bite of my hot dog, burning the roof of my mouth, and plunge back into the mass of people. I tap the toe of my boots on the grass as I walk, dislodging the onions. It's dark, the air nipped with autumn cold, and the flames of the fire eaters burst in glowing pillars over the heads of the crowd.

I take one look at those flames and change course.

I'm not in the mood for Kamran Lajani.

Frantic drums sound from the big top tent on the edge of the carnival. I stare at it for a moment, almost sick with longing. Lit up against the night sky, it looms over the grounds, calling to us and watching over us like our own temple. It's striped midnight blue and lilac, a creature of the night like us, blending in with the shadowed mountain peaks all around.

I should be in there right now; I should be on that trapeze. Soaring weightless over the crowd, twisting and swinging, buoyed by their gasps. Chalk coating my palms and crammed under my nails. Sweat slicking my skin.

I grunt and tuck my cast to my chest, shoving the last of the hot dog in my mouth.

Soon. Then I'll show these townies what's up.

I hate to go in there when I can't perform, but I head for the gaping mouth of the big top. Robbie keeps a watchful eye over the whole carnival, but he's especially careful with the circus acts. The performers put their lives on the line with every single performance. There are no safety nets and hidden lines here. We do this for real.

Even though it's his damn circus, Robbie fucking hates the risks. When Yan dropped me three weeks ago—dropped me in all the possible ways—I became a prime example of the perils of aerial work.

Robbie won't be happy to see me back so soon. Well, tough shit.

I veer away from the bustling main entrance, around the side of the tent. There's always a slit or two in the canvas, left behind by roadies so they can haul equipment in and out. Finding a gap in the heavy cloth, I duck inside, moist heat washing over me like I'm stepping into a greenhouse. My duffel catches on the flap as I move deeper inside and I lurch, instinctively flexing my hand in my cast. Burning pain lashes through my wrist, and I blink away the tears brimming in my eyes.

Damn tent.

Damn wrist.

Damn piece-of-shit duffel.

I clear my throat and straighten my shoulders, though no one can see me here in the shadows. Keeping to the edge of the crowds, I circle around the big top interior.

Robbie is exactly where I knew he'd be. He stands with his boots planted and his arms crossed, eyes glued on the performer spinning overhead. I glance up, following his line of sight—it's Aleksi, our headliner. The face on all our posters—and what a face. I used to love watching him work, gasping at the fluid way he spun on the silks like a spider weaving a web.

But Aleksi is the spitting image of his brother Yan, and the sight of him now makes the hot dog lurch in my stomach.

Doesn't matter. I duck my head and make a beeline for the man in charge. If any visitors were to glance at Robbie, they'd probably think he was a roadie. He's young: early thirties with sandy blond hair and scruff on his chin. He dresses all in faded black—thick work pants and a long-sleeved t-shirt. A tool belt hangs around his hips, and a radio crackles on the belt.

He looks unimportant. A small cog in a vast machine.

First rule of the carnival: appearances can be deceiving. He's not just some roadie. Robbie's our puppet master.

"Hey, boss." I give him my most winning smile as I plant myself square in front of him. Better not to dance around the point—I came back uninvited.

Robbie's eyes flick down, and irritation ripples across his face. He lowers his chin to stare me down, jaw clenching.

"Did I say you could come back?"

His Scottish accent always makes him sound softer than he really is.

"Probably not," I say cheerfully, dropping my duffel at his feet. "But I got this sixth sense. Figured you missed me."

"You figured wrong." Robbie nudges my bag with his boot,

nose wrinkling like I've brought him a dead mouse. "You messed yourself up. You can't work like that, Hazel."

He means my busted wrist; the bones still throbbing in my cast. I know he's right, that there's no reason for him to house and feed me while I can't even perform, but there is no way on this planet I'm about to turn tail and slink off back to the cornfields.

"I'll work a stand. Hook-a-Duck or some shit." I force another smile, trying not to let the hurt reach my face. I know Robbie's my boss and he doesn't owe me shit, but it's cold for him to dismiss me like that. Like I hurt myself because I was careless, not like a cheating scumbag literally dropped me.

Like this isn't my home just as much as his.

Come on, man, I urge him in my brain. *Muster up an emotion.*

Robbie looks at me, face as blank as a marble statue, then slides his gaze back up to Aleksi.

"Fine," he mutters, not even looking at me anymore. "But you'll earn your keep, same as everyone else."

Asshole. I never said I wouldn't, and I resent the implication. But I keep my face carefully blank to match his, leaning down to scoop up my duffel.

"Always a pleasure, boss man."

Robbie rolls his eyes without even looking down.

Autumn Tricksters is available solo or as part of the Year of the Harem box set.

126

About the Author

Kayla Wren is a British author who writes romance with heat and heart. She loves Reverse Harem, Enemies-to-Lovers, and Forbidden Love tropes.

Kayla writes prickly men with hearts of gold, secretly-sexy geeks, and—best of all—she's ALWAYS had a thing for the villains.

You can connect with me on:
- https://www.kaylawrenauthor.com
- https://www.bookbub.com/authors/kayla-wren
- https://www.amazon.com/~/e/B08CL281V1

Subscribe to my newsletter:
- https://www.kaylawrenauthor.com/newsletter

Also by Kayla Wren

Year of the Harem Collection:
Lords of Summer
Autumn Tricksters
Knights of Winter
Spring Kings

Standalone titles:
The Naughty List
Roomies

The Office Hours trilogy:
Extra Credit
Bonus Study
After Class

www.ingramcontent.com/pod-product-compliance
Lightning Source LLC
Chambersburg PA
CBHW052002170626
46808CB00007B/2745